"The Casting Couch Is Closed for the Season."

Shelley was smugly pleased when David gaped at her momentarily before breaking into bemused laughter. "Don't even think of using your famous charm on me."

"You saw through me," he said. "I did hope to see the script, find out how you've handled the character, and maybe determine my chances of nabbing the role. As for using my charm, well, forgive me for saying so, but it's a pleasure to exercise my charm on you, whether or not I get the part."

"Don't call me, someone will call you."

EVA CLAIRE
is a portrait artist and musician who paints pictures and composes symphonies in her novels of romantic love and commitment. She and her husband travel to research her novels and make their home in the beautiful Ohio Valley.

Dear Reader:

Romance readers have been enthusiastic about Silhouette Special Editions for years. And that's not by accident: Special Editions were the first of their kind and continue to feature realistic stories with heightened romantic tension.

The longer stories, sophisticated style, greater sensual detail and variety that made Special Editions popular are the same elements that will make you want to read book after book.

We hope that you enjoy this Special Edition today, and will enjoy many more.

The Editors at Silhouette Books

EVA CLAIRE
Star
Attraction

Silhouette Special Edition

Published by Silhouette Books New York

America's Publisher of Contemporary Romance

Silhouette Books by Eva Claire

Appalachian Summer (SE #149)
Star Attraction (SE #240)

SILHOUETTE BOOKS
300 E. 42nd St., New York, N.Y. 10017

Copyright © 1985 by Claire DeLong

Distributed by Pocket Books

ISBN: 0-373-09240-7

First Silhouette Books printing May, 1985

10 9 8 7 6 5 4 3 2 1

Map by Ray Lundgren

America's Publisher of Contemporary Romance

Printed in the U.S.A.
BC91

To Mary Clare,
with sincere gratitude for
believing in me from the
very beginning.

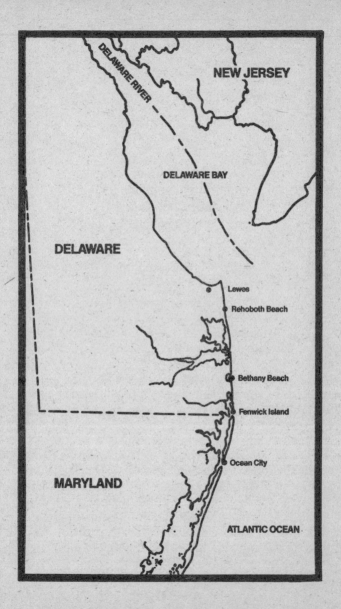

Chapter One

Strolling along the warm sand of the beach, Shelley considered the seemingly calm surface of the Atlantic. Before her appreciative dark eyes, the water that seemed glassy-slick, reflecting the cloudless blue of the sky above, was transformed. Far out in the ocean gentle ripples silently formed, gathered momentum and brought waves of cool sea water inland to splash against the waiting sand.

Gazing out over the ocean, Shelley found herself comparing the changes taking place there with the changes in her own life—changes that sometimes seemed beyond her control. Before coming to this lovely beach property on the Delaware coast, she had known highs and lows, dealt with indecision, overcome inhibitions and sunk into deep despair. The blissful tranquillity around her contrasted sharply with her past as she recalled the tumultuous years of living life in the fast lane in a futile effort to be something, someone she was not, years filled with anxiety and heartache, disappointments and shattered dreams.

Casting off the unpleasant memories and sighing appreciatively, Shelley allowed herself to bask in the peaceful summer warmth while she savored the silence embracing her, the only sounds the lapping of waves licking at the shoreline and the occasional caw of a water bird swooping over the landscape.

Since renting the furnished cottage on an unoccupied beachfront estate, there had been nothing to intrude upon her privacy or interrupt her solitude, no unexpected interferences to mar this precious opportunity to commune with nature and attempt to rebuild her life.

"Come, boys! Here, Karl! Come, Fritz!"

Shelley's reverie was interrupted by the sound of an unfamiliar masculine voice accompanied by the excited barking of dogs, a barking that grew louder and louder behind her.

Disconcerted, Shelley spun about. Her eyes narrowed under the brilliant rays of the sun, and she lifted one hand to shade her eyes. The beach was private and posted against trespassers. Who, then, she asked herself, would dare to invade the area? And allow dogs to run on someone else's property?

And then Shelley saw them—two sleek dogs moving at breakneck speed, their long slender legs bringing them across the shimmering sand to the spot where she stood. Dobermans!

"They are just dogs," she chided herself aloud.

But within her an agitated voice kept up the warning. These were not just dogs; these were Dobermans.

And with each passing instant, they were moving closer . . . closer . . . coming so close that she could see their gaping jaws, their long gleaming white teeth.

"Hold! Come!"

Ignoring the sharp commands, the magnificent black and tan beasts continued to sprint across the sand on a collision course with Shelley's frozen frame.

Shelley never looked at the man. Her eyes, her attention, her fear centered on those black beauties moving with such effortless grace, closing the gap that separated her from them. Bracing herself for the inevitable, she closed her eyes and waited . . . and waited. Cautiously opening one eye, she saw that they had come to a panting halt before her, saliva dripping from their pink tongues onto her bare feet.

"Go away! Scat!" she croaked, then added beseechingly, "Please!" She forced herself to look into the dogs' glittering eyes, trying to gauge their intention. "Please go!" she squeaked. Frustrated tears sprang to her eyes, misting her vision.

"Don't frighten the lady, boys! Sit! Stay! Good boys."

The huskily masculine voice won a response from the dogs, who promptly sat back on their haunches in an attitude of waiting watchfulness. She had the feeling that they sensed her fear and were amused by it; for Shelley, it was no laughing matter.

Warily, her glance shifted from the dogs to the man. A grateful comment formed on her numb lips as, through tear-starred lashes, she gazed at the blurred image moving toward her and sucked in her breath once more.

"Chris!" she cried.

How had he found her? Why, after three years, had he wanted to? More importantly, who among her small circle of close friends had betrayed her by informing Christopher Devon of her whereabouts? And why now, when things were going so well for her? Her chest felt tight, clogged with emotion as she continued to observe the tall, lithe man walking with an elegance of motion until only a few yards separated them.

Blinking back her tears in an effort to clear her eyes, Shelley forced her gaze to focus on his features and knew a moment of doubt.

The thick hair framing the tanned face was lighter, more of a russet gold than the gleaming blackish brown she recalled, but it was probably a trick of the sun or a good dye job—Chris's incredible vanity would have permitted such a change, she reminded herself. Although she expected his face would reflect the ravages of time and his undoubted debauchery, his features were still as classically perfect as she remembered . . . or were they? High smooth forehead, firm square jaw, sensual lips, the lower a bit fuller than the top . . . and his eyes . . . She couldn't see his eyes because of the large mirrored sunglasses protecting them from the sun's bright glare, but Shelley was certain they would be piercing jewels of jet.

"Get off this property!" she cried angrily, her indignation at his abrupt reappearance in her orderly life overcoming the fear she had experienced at first sight of the dogs. "I'm warning you!"

"Warning me?"

"This is private property. If I were you, I'd leave now before it's too late," she suggested, folding her arms purposefully over her heaving chest, which seemed to have captured his bemused attention.

"What will happen if I don't leave and it gets—what did you say?—too late?" he countered in a low, throbbingly male voice that seemed subtly different from the voice Shelley recalled as belonging to Christopher Devon, the man she had once loved to distraction but who was now the last person in the world she wanted to encounter.

His beautifully shaped head swung in the direction of the main house, splendid and imposing with its rich cedar siding and large windows facing onto the Atlantic. Seizing the opportunity to observe him closely, Shelley considered the possibility that he had been on the beach for some time, waiting and watching; perhaps he had seen the caretakers leave for town about an hour ago. Maybe he knew, as so many of the Rehoboth Beach residents knew, that the owner of this spectacular estate was never in residence and therefore she was now alone and defenseless.

Christopher Devon, Shelley reminded herself, was capable of anything. Certainly, he wouldn't think twice about tracking down a woman who

· had once rejected him, especially if she was now successful and financially secure.

Shelley studied the uncommonly attractive face. It was Chris, wasn't it? she quizzed herself as doubt began to nag at her.

"What will happen if I don't leave as you ask?" he repeated, his lips curving in a teasing smile that was subtly different from Chris Devon's insolent grin. "Will I turn into a pumpkin? Or will my dogs become harnessed horses to pull my golden coach?"

"I'll have you run off!" she replied angrily. She unfolded her arms and balled her hands into fists. Spying the gesture, the dogs growled. "Call off your dogs!"

"Why should I?"

"Because you . . . they . . . are trespassing."

"So you said." He paused to consider her. "Just whose property is this?" As he asked the question, his right hand extended in a slight gesture that silenced the disturbed growling of the dogs.

Drawing herself up to her full five feet five inches, Shelley said proudly, "*I* live here."

"You own the property?" Doubt laced the inquiry.

He was watching her closely, and though she could not see his eyes, she could see her own reflection in the mirrored glasses. It wasn't exactly an impressive image, she had to admit. Having become accustomed to her solitude, she had given up all pretension and took little pains with her appearance; when she and Chris had been together, she had spent hours making herself presentable. Dressed now in short cut-off denims and a comfortable white knit halter top, she could easily be mistaken for a beach bum with her tumbled shoulder-length sable hair, scrubbed face devoid of cosmetics and freckled by the sun, to say nothing of her unshod feet encrusted with sand.

And why did that bother her? she asked herself. In the past, Chris had frequently seen her unkempt and without makeup—without clothes at all, for that matter, she recalled ruefully.

But it did bother her. And it began to bother her more as she slowly came to realize that this self-assured individual was not Christopher Devon. Despite the close resemblance, there were too many glaring differences. It wasn't just the color of his hair, the smooth unlined texture of his tanned skin that was too youthful, the strangely warm personality, the oddly teasing lilt in his voice that wasn't quite the same as she remembered, that dimple in his chin . . . and the two each side of his shapely mouth . . .

Chris had never had dimples!

Oh, Lord, she groaned inwardly, this isn't Chris Devon! What had she said to him? And what was he saying to her? Absorbed in her rude examination of him, she had become hypnotized by the timbre of his voice without listening to what he was saying.

"I'm sorry, what did you say?" she asked.

"I asked if you are an animal lover?"

"Why?"

He laughed. It was a merry sound that lifted Shelley's embarrassed spirits and brought a warm flush to her cheeks. "Fritz and Karl seem quite content with you. They're lying at your feet, quiet as mice."

Shelley eyed the dogs curiously. Just as he had said, they were at her feet, their sleek bodies stretched full length in an attitude of relaxation. Tentatively, experimentally, she unclenched her right fist, extending the fingers downward. Immediately, one dark head lifted, and a rough tongue darted out to lick at her offered hand in a gesture of affection.

"See?" he asked, chuckling softly. "Karl likes you. Fritz senses that there is nothing to fear from you. May I assume that I can be equally fearless?"

"I always had animals around me until I came here." Her reflective words were wistful. "Oh, there was the time I lived in that fancy apartment . . . pets weren't allowed, not even a goldfish or a parakeet . . ," Her voice drifted off as she realized that she was saying too much, babbling inanely to this man who was a stranger.

"Just who are you?" she blurted.

"Who am I?" he asked. "I should be asking who you are!" he said in that seductive voice that was charming her out of her discomfort. Chris's voice had never had such depth or that lilting quality that made this man's voice unique and sensually disturbing. When Shelley offered no response to his question, he said, "Let's put it this way: I've been running along my beach with my dogs. Suddenly, you appear out of nowhere—"

"I didn't come from nowhere," Shelley interrupted. "I came from that cottage back there. That's where I live. Nobody lives in the big house . . . except the caretakers," she added quickly, anxious to assert her right to be on the beach.

"Ah! Then you're my guest?"

"Your guest?" Shelley echoed.

His head nodded. As he allowed his implication to sink into her befuddled brain, a bemused smile curved his lips. "It seems that neither of us is trespassing, hmm?"

"I rented the cottage through the Stevens Real Estate Agency," Shelley said, comprehending that this stunning individual was the absent owner of the property upon which she was now living. "My friend, Darby Webster, works for the agency. She handled the lease . . ."

"Ah, yes!" he said in an amused tone. "The Stevens Agency and Darby Webster." With long square-tipped fingers, he removed the silvery sunglasses to reveal eyes of a startling blue green, almond shaped and glinting with merriment as they met Shelley's disbelieving glance.

"You're the owner." Shelley's monotone was neither a statement nor a question, but a dull acceptance of his identity.

"I'm still waiting for you to tell me who you are," he remarked patiently.

Shelley wasn't listening. She was remembering the Andersons, Velma and Harry, the cheery elderly couple who cared for the property. A few hours ago they had come to inform her that they were going into town to stock supplies; why hadn't she realized that the mere mention of stocking supplies meant the owner's arrival was imminent?

"Your name, young lady?" he was asking with teasing patience.

Inexplicably tongue-tied, Shelley did not immediately reply. Things were happening too fast. First, there had been the unwelcome sight of the dogs, then the hurtful memories of Chris and now this startling development. Her precious solitude, she realized, was a thing of the past; the owner had returned to take up residence.

"I'm waiting," he remarked. "Are you going to tell me who you are, or must I contact the real estate agency?"

Squaring her shoulders and lifting her chin, Shelley took a deep breath and let it out. "I'm Shelley Tremayne," she announced, waiting for the raised eyebrows, the twinkle of recognition, the exclamations of awe that customarily followed the voicing of her name. His only reaction was a gentle curving of his lips in acknowledgment.

"That didn't hurt a bit, did it?"

Shelley met his bemused blue green eyes. Realizing that her name seemed to mean nothing to him, she felt relief flood over her like a cascading waterfall. Her meteoric rise to fame had become a burden, and finding someone to whom she was not a celebrity was welcome.

"Is there a Mr. Tremayne?" he asked.

"Mr. Tremayne is my father. He doesn't live here."

"No husband." It was a smug statement rather than a question. "A lover, perhaps, to share the moonlit summer nights?"

The nerve of the man! Shelley fumed. Even the owner of the property had no right to stab at her personal life.

Nevertheless, she responded to his insinuation. "No lovers." Before he could pose another ill-mannered question, she asked, "Why the inquisition? I pay my rent through the agency, and they pass it on to you, don't they? What I do and how I live my life shouldn't concern you."

His disarming smile broadened, bringing the deep dimples into play. "I had forgotten that I'd listed the guesthouse with the rental agency, but your charming presence has effectively reminded me. As I recall, I specified that the cottage was to be leased to a proper person or persons."

"Just what is that supposed to mean?"

Surveying her in silence, his beautiful eyes skimmed her shapely body, their sharpness making her uncomfortably aware of the scantiness of her attire, her rumpled appearance. Adjusting the halter top with one hand while the other tugged at the ragged ends of the shorts, Shelley knew that her casual clothing revealed altogether too much.

"Since I am seldom in residence—," he began.

"All the more reason why you shouldn't care who rents the cottage so long as they keep it in good condition and pay their rent!" Shelley interrupted.

"I have a reputation to consider. It is imperative that nothing, no breath of scandal or unsavory companions, be connected with me."

"Scandal! Unsavory companions!" Shelley exploded. "I beg your pardon—"

"And I beg yours," he said, lifting one cautionary hand before he went on easily, "I had hoped to rent to a quiet elderly couple, or perhaps someone cultured or artistic."

"And what makes you think I'm not quiet?" she demanded to know. "Or cultured? Or artistic?" Had her name registered with him, he would have known that she was a former news reporter now turned novelist; he would have recognized her as the celebrated author of a best-selling novel now being considered for a major motion picture, efforts considered rather artistic in most circles.

"Why have you rented the cottage?" he asked, his tone soft and interested. His accompanying smile was dazzling.

"It's exactly the sort of place I need for my work," she answered, despising herself for responding to the warmth of his smile. "Quiet and off the beaten track."

"Ah!" he sighed with resignation. "That's what's worrying me."

"I don't understand."

"Your work, sand urchin. What do you do that requires the isolation of the beach?" He paused, fixing her with an unblinking stare that spoke volumes.

Shelley grunted. "I can imagine what you think I do," she mumbled. His assessing glance told her he had concluded she was a woman of loose morals whose work was the sort normally conducted on street corners in the dark of night.

Perversely, she did not wish to correct his assumptions.

"I also find the beach restful." His voice was quiet, contained and hypnotizingly husky. "I like the privacy and isolation. In my line of work, I need a quiet place like this. That's why I bought this strip of land and had the house built. The guesthouse was an afterthought. I have friends who like to come here, and I don't like to turn them away. But after a few days they begin to annoy me with their chatter, the parties . . ."

Listening raptly, Shelley found herself entranced with his melodic voice. It was mesmerizing, rich and full, liltingly delightful. Chris's voice had been deep and mellow, the bombastic voice of an actor, but he had never attained the resonance that was an inherent part of this man's voice, a resonance that caused goose pimples to form at the nape of her neck.

Clearing her throat, she asked, "What do you do that requires privacy?"

Brazenly, her glance roamed over his handsome face and down his lanky frame in much the same way he had been studying her. She considered the ways he could earn a living that would require privacy and yet permit him to be so physically fit. He had to be involved in some form of outdoor pursuit. An athlete, perhaps? Certainly, whatever he did was lucrative, she reasoned. Only the very wealthy could afford the exclusive Rehoboth Beach properties.

"I meditate, read a lot," he replied evasively, offering no hint of his line of work.

"For a living?" she blurted. Whom did he think he was kidding?

"It helps me in what I do," was his enigmatic reply.

Shelley sighed and turned to study the wispy clouds forming along the distant horizon. "I've told you my name, but I still don't know yours. Would you mind telling it to me?" she asked.

He smiled engagingly. "It must have been on your lease. It would have been toward the top, near your own name."

"I didn't pay any attention," Shelley admitted. "Why don't you tell it to me?" His secretive amusement was infectious, and her question was laced with mischievous laughter.

His eyes danced but he said nothing. Shelley began to wonder why he was being deliberately obtuse. Was he turning the tables on her, imitating her own reluctance to reveal her name?

Shelley smiled charmingly and coaxed, "Please?"

To her amazement, he bowed from the waist and swept an imaginary hat from his head. His arm cut the air in an arc as he rose to military attention and said, "David Warren at your service, fair lady."

Although he seemed to be expecting some sort of reaction, Shelley simply gazed blankly into his grinning face. "Why do I get the feeling that I should be impressed?" she asked, while somewhere in the recesses of her brain, the name registered dimly. Who was he? Someone famous, she was certain, as she tried to remember where she had seen or heard the name. It had been recently, she knew, but where?

His brows rose in question. His lips twitched

as if he were having difficulty restraining himself. "You've never heard that name before?" he asked with seeming casualness.

"It's a rather ordinary name," she remarked while continuing to search her memory bank for clues. With his eyes fixed intently on her, it was difficult to think logically.

As if satisfied with her reply, he leaned forward and murmured conspiratorially, "Let's keep it our secret, then, shall we?"

"Secret? From whom?" He was a most exasperating individual, she concluded, full of enigmatic remarks and evasive replies to perfectly logical questions. He must be very famous, she concluded, wishing she could recall whatever it was she knew about him.

"I am well known," he said quietly, as though he were sharing some deep dark secret. "There are lots of people who would invade this beach, No Trespassing signs notwithstanding, if they knew of my presence here. I can't allow that to happen. Please bear that in mind."

"You sound as though you think I'm going to race to the telephone and call everyone I know to tell them I've rented a cottage from David Warren," she commented, her humor coming to the fore to lend a teasing touch to her words.

"It wouldn't be the first time."

"From someone renting the cottage?"

He nodded gravely.

"Then why rent it at all?" she asked.

"Why not? I'm seldom here."

"You shouldn't be here now." At his questioning glance, Shelley added hastily, "I mean, I was told I'd be alone here. Except for the care-takers, of course. Why are you here now?" she asked.

"Actually, I'm here for a bit of R and R be-tween jobs."

"Well, I won't bother you," she assured him. "I have my own work to do. It's very demanding."

"I'm sure it is." He managed to sound sincere, she noticed.

"A perfect pair, aren't we?" Shelley laughed. "I mean, we're standing here in the hot sun, sizing each other up like two gladiators squaring off in the arena, each unwilling to reveal any-thing specific to the other . . ." Her wry words drifted off when she spied the small frown creas-ing his brow.

"This is a bit silly, isn't it?" he said, flashing a warm smile. "Since we're going to be sharing this property, what do you say we call a truce?" At her answering smile of acceptance, he con-tinued, "I won't be here long, so let's establish the ground rules, shall we?"

"Rules?" she parroted. What now? she groaned inwardly. Just when things were set-tling down, he has to go and spoil it all!

Shifting his weight, David assumed a deter-mined stance and his eyes rested on Shelley's face. He was still smiling but his eyes were shadowed. Shelley resigned herself to hearing him out, if for no other reason than to hear that marvelous voice of his, which was doing strange things to her nervous system.

"I'll take your word for it that you have a lease," he began, and Shelley's quick temper took hold.

"I'll get it!" she cried out.

When she would have spun on her heel and raced to the cottage, she was halted by his fingers, warm and strong, clasping her wrist. Stunned by the sudden contact, she stood mutely gazing up into his face while a delightful shiver of warmth spread up her arm from the wrist he held.

"Don't bother. I'll take your word, I said. I will also appreciate it if you confine yourself to your cottage while I'm here. I don't want you coming to the main house or imposing on me in any way."

"Is that rule one of your ground rules?" she ground out between pursed lips.

"Rule two is that I will not tolerate drunkenness or disorderliness."

"I suppose that means no orgies?" Shelley asked with mock solemnity.

A dark glance was his only response, although he released his hold on her wrist and his firm lips twitched in a hint of a smile.

"Rule three," he intoned. "Under no circumstances are you to force yourself on me, try to be photographed with me or otherwise invade my privacy. This is my home and it is my castle."

Shelley gazed at him curiously. Bringing her hands up before her, she began to applaud, slowly and dramatically. "Bravo! Sir Laurence Olivier couldn't have given a better delivery," she said in sarcastic admiration. "Your speech was delivered with such convincing dramatic passion."

"I beg your pardon?"

"Have you ever considered the stage?" Shelley

asked. "You really should, you know. Your voice is magnificent. I'll bet you could be heard in the very last row of the largest theater on Broadway."

He seemed momentarily embarrassed. Regaining his poise, he tossed back his head and laughed. Then, sobering, he said, "There is one other thing."

"Oh, do let's hear it!"

"I don't want you annoying or teasing my dogs."

"Who, me?" Shelley swallowed and slanted a glance at the sleeping dogs lying at her feet. "I'm terrified of Dobermans. I can't imagine annoying them or teasing them."

"They may take to hanging about your cottage," he said. "If they become troublesome, just send them home."

"Send them home? How?"

His jewellike glance impaled her. "You'll undoubtedly think of some way," he remarked with assurance. "Dobermans are an odd breed. Loyal, devoted—"

"And vicious!" finished Shelley. "Don't forget vicious!"

His quizzical glance rested on the pulse beating heavily at the base of her throat; disturbed by the touch of his eyes on her flesh, Shelley placed one hand over the pulse in hopes of disguising her unnatural fear as she remembered the one supreme act of viciousness she had seen perpetrated by this breed of dog.

"My brother . . . he was only five . . . he was attacked by a Doberman," she said haltingly. "It was very frightening to watch. I've never forgotten it."

"I am sorry," he said with genuine compassion. "Your brother, is he . . . I mean . . .?"

"He's fine. A bit scarred in the arms and legs, but he lived to tell about the ordeal. He's an attorney in Ann Arbor, Michigan, has a wife and three children." What was there about this man that caused her to babble on so? Shelley wondered. It wasn't at all like her.

"I don't think you have anything to fear from Fritz and Karl," David stated reassuringly. "They like you and will probably be as loyal to you as they are to me. I wonder how you managed that?"

Shelley shrugged. "My inherent goodness, no doubt. Animals know about those things," she commented mischievously.

David's glittering glance swept her skimpily clad body, caressed the rosiness of her complexion, the tumbled curtain of her hair. "That may be true."

"Thank you. I doubt that you intended that remark as a compliment, but I'll take it as one nevertheless," Shelley said.

"Then you'll agree to my conditions?"

"Do I have a choice?"

"Not really."

"Then, of course, I will agree," Shelley said with a saccharine smile. "I should tell you that I do have a few close friends who visit me on occasion. They are professional people. Some are even into the arts and culture." She could not resist voicing the verbal jab. "We all like music, by the way, and enjoy a hearty laugh. Do you think that will annoy you?" Impish laughter laced her solemn remarks.

"I enjoy music myself," he replied.

What sort of music did he like? she found herself wondering. Since he had claimed to be heavily into reading and meditation, his musical taste probably ran to the classics.

"About the dogs, Ms. Tremayne," he said, his voice slicing through her ruminations. "They are guard dogs and will probably take to guarding you. Please try not to be alarmed by their presence."

"I'll try," she mumbled.

His sun-browned hand was extended toward her. Shelley reluctantly placed her small hand in his, sealing their verbal agreement with a handshake. Again she felt a thrill of excitement as his fingers closed about hers. Sensing that she had been bested, she murmured something unintelligible, tugged her hand free and turned on her heel to make her way back to the cottage.

From the relative safety of her patio, she glanced back at the regal figure of David Warren jogging down the beach. At his side, the two dogs frolicked; the trio presented a magnificent spectacle of natural beauty.

Inhaling the salt breeze wafting inland from the sea, Shelley feasted her eyes on David's rapidly disappearing frame. The man was a tone poem of precise movements and elegance, she mused, observing the way his long legs carried him over the sand with fluid grace and assurance. Again she pondered his occupation and yearned to remember where she had come across his name. He wasn't an athlete, she concluded, for the sports pages were not high on her list of preferred reading. At one time, she had been forced to scan them, to glean facts and figures about star performers in advance of an interview. But now she was free to choose her own reading matter, and she reveled in the new freedom.

Shelley watched David until he was nothing more than a hazy mirage blending with the horizon. Expelling an appreciative sigh, she turned away from the sight that had been tugging at her heart. Her cheeks were still warm from the heated encounter with the man who so closely resembled Christopher Devon. Both men were unusually handsome, but Shelley knew that Chris had used his good looks to conceal a devious nature. As for David Warren, Shelley knew nothing whatever about him, but in those few minutes on the beach she had sensed that he was a man who could be trusted, who possessed a sense of humor; hadn't he laughed at himself when she had turned her teasing tongue on him, taunted him about his artificial and overly dramatic way of presenting himself?

Once again her thoughts churned as she considered the man. She tried to recall everything Darby Webster had told her about the absent owner, but could remember only Darby's gushing remarks about his wealth and prestige, along with the promise that Shelley would not be troubled with his presence since he seldom had time to stay at the beach property. His name must have been mentioned, but she was certain Darby had been vague about his occupation.

"This is madness!" she announced to the empty room, then continued to berate herself silently. Have you forgotten your promise to avoid getting involved in personal relationships until the script is finished? And how about those promises you made to Lord David? Why are you wasting time and energy fantasizing over a strange man who piques your curiosity? A man who uncannily resembles Chris Devon, she added grimly. That resemblance alone ought to turn you off.

Abandoning the disturbing thoughts of David Warren, Shelley turned her attention to her work. It was no easy task, she was learning, to write a faithful screenplay of her best-selling novel, the first novel she had ever written.

And there were those videotapes to study, she remembered with a jolt; videotapes of talented performers, given to her for the express purpose of helping her select actors to portray her fictional characters. Having fought a hard fight for the right to choose the cast, an honor seldom allowed a mere author, it would be a dreadful mistake to botch the job through divided interest and murky concentration.

Filled with resolve, Shelley moved to the television set, turned it on and touched her index finger to the controls of the VCR. Snuggling down in the roomy chair facing the television, she reached for the glass of tea sitting on the end table alongside her pad and pen. She lifted the glass to her lips and made a sound of disgust as she realized that the ice had long ago melted, leaving a warm and decidedly tasteless liquid in the glass.

For a moment Shelley considered going to the kitchen for a fresh drink, but then her attention was drawn to the images flickering on the screen. A promo preceding the film itself offered tantalizing clips from the movie, while a disembodied voice promised a gripping tale of love and adventure.

"At least it's historical and in color," she remarked aloud, appreciatively eyeing the colorful costumes before her.

When the screen filled with a tight close-up, Shelley was certain her imagination was playing tricks on her, that she was still fantasizing about the man she had just met. Surely that was the only explanation for what she thought she was seeing.

But the classically beautiful face filling the twenty-five-inch screen was real and all too familiar. Glowing blue green eyes glittered, the dimpled smile taunted and the unseen announcer's voice declared that this was the actor of a lifetime, in the role of a lifetime.

"David Warren stars in a tale of danger, of deceit and treachery, of a love that changed the course of history. David Warren is the Welsh commoner Owen Tudor, Master of the Costume, lover to a queen, rival of a king. This is David Warren as you've never seen him before, in a love story you'll never forget!"

Chapter Two

After the initial shock of discovery, Shelley leaned forward to study the television screen closely. No wonder the name had seemed familiar, she chided herself—David Warren, like Christopher Devon, was an actor! His name had been on the list submitted to her by the studio casting office, and his films were among those she had been given for consideration. And David Warren wasn't just an actor; he was one of the leading lights of the theatrical world. In her days of glory as a talk-show interviewer, his name had been dropped with the same easy nonchalance as the latest fashion craze from Paris.

Relaxing in the chair, Shelley held a silent conversation with herself as she sought to understand her inability to recognize the celebrated David Warren.

She remembered that there had been trouble with the studio from the very beginning. The studio had desperately wanted the rights to the novel, but they were reluctant to hand over cast selection to an inexperienced first-time novelist. After months of haggling and a bit of pressure from the high-powered literary agency handling the novel, Shelley had won the right to pick her own cast. Even then, the studio casting people had subtly sought to keep the upper hand by submitting names they considered suitable in the hope that Shelley would bow to their superior wisdom. The arguments from the casting personnel became unbearable, but Shelley stood firm, compromised on nothing. When she boldly rejected all the names suggested, they attempted to win her by offering a number of videocassettes for her to view. Shelley set aside all those featuring star performers; she had decided that she preferred unknowns for the film version of her novel. When all else failed, she told herself, she would consider name stars, but only then.

But none of the up-and-coming actors had impressed her. Feeling that the studio had won, she was now being forced to view the films of top actors, among them the works of David Warren, whose name, like so many others, Shelley had managed to forget as she tried to judge on performance rather than celebrity status. She reminded herself that when she placed a cassette into the slot of the VCR, she didn't even bother to check the cast. The film now flickering across the screen had been chosen at random, without thought or particular care, she realized.

Still, she argued silently, she should have recognized Warren's name. Perhaps, Shelley rationalized, she hadn't really wanted to admit to herself that the man she had met on the beach was a popular superstar. He was certainly, not what she thought a star of his magnitude would be. A superstar such as David Warren should be older, larger than life, immune from the everyday necessities of life such as exercising dogs on the beach. He should be a pompous, arrogant individual, not a likable young man in his thirties with a devastating smile and delightful sense of humor.

While Shelley was reflecting on her landlord's identity, the film had begun. Almost unwillingly, she found her attention drawn to the screen, and then she was caught up in the story unfolding before her, absorbed in the intrigue and passion being played out by a troupe of experienced actors. She completely forgot about David Warren, the man and the actor, as she sat entranced and slightly breathless, waiting for the outcome of the convoluted story based on historical truth.

As the film progressed, Shelley found herself cheering for Owen Tudor, the Welshman who had captured the heart of a queen whose husband cared more for battles and glory than for his lovely bride. The clashes between the handsome Master of the Costume and the belligerent warrior-king found Shelley holding her breath as if she were actually an eyewitness to those heated confrontations. During the tastefully performed love scenes, she sighed wistfully, wanting only the best for this couple who, in the heat of an all-consuming love, threw caution to the winds and ultimately introduced the Welsh name of Tudor into the British monarchy.

When the final scene had been played and the film came to a conclusion, Shelley sat gazing at the dark screen, feeling bereft that the magic was no more. Gradually, reality closed about her, and she remembered her teasing words to David Warren: "Have you ever considered the stage?" No wonder he laughed so heartily, she told herself, recalling his amused response to her teasing taunts.

In the midst of her merriment, Shelley found herself reflecting on the performance she had just witnessed. David Warren was not, she realized, just another actor playing a role; he had brought life to the portrayal and made dry history excitingly real. His abilities were unquestionably rare, his reputation justly deserved.

In a sudden burst of energy, Shelley began to sort through the videocassettes stacked beside the tape machine, seeking another film featuring David Warren. She was not disappointed, for there were several. Throughout the gold-washed sunset hours, she gazed raptly at her television screen, immersed in the many performances of the talented actor, each in its own way more exciting, more memorable than the one before.

It was well after midnight when she at last turned off the television, showered, and fell wearily into bed to dream of a man with glowing aquamarine eyes and a smile accented by endearing dimples.

In the sun-splashed hours following dawn, Shelley awoke with one thought blazing like a flame in her mind: David Warren was the actor she wanted to portray the hero in her film. He alone, she felt, would be able to breathe life into the complex character of Lord D'Arcy, make him seem real and likable so that he would be emblazoned for all time upon the minds and memories of all who saw the motion picture.

All through breakfast and after, Shelley's thoughts returned over and over to the intriguing man whom she had met and spoken with the day before. Questions scampered through her mind as she drank her morning coffee and gazed curiously at the impressive main house, anxious for a glimpse of David Warren.

Some of her thoughts, centered on the similarities between David Warren and Christopher Devon; since both were actors, she began to consider whether Warren's reaction to her identity was as innocent and honest as she had believed. A consummate actor such as Warren would have known how to appear unimpressed or even unaware of Shelley's famous name while in actuality being fully cognizant not only of her identity, but of the fact that her first work of fiction was being translated to the screen. He would have known that an intensive search was being made for actors and actresses to bring the steamy tale to vibrant life. He might even be aware of her battle with the studio for the right to choose those actors and actresses.

Perhaps, she mused, he was like Chris in more ways than mere physical resemblance. Chris, she knew from hard experience, kept a sharp eye out for opportunities to further his career; surely David Warren would do the same. A leading actor who wanted a prime role in a forthcoming motion picture and who had the means to get it would certainly have no qualms about doing whatever was necessary to secure it, would he?

And what about Darby Webster? What part had she played in this small drama? She knew Shelley's reason for needing a place like the beach cottage to complete the script. Surely she had known of Warren's notoriety as well.

Needing proof of her assumptions, Shelley rose from the kitchen chair and made her way to the screened patio overlooking the quiet beach. As if on cue, David Warren appeared, strolling blithely along the stretch of sand. His magnificent physique, haloed by the morning sun, seemed etched against the tranquil landscape by some unseen hand.

As she watched, his head swung in the direction of the cottage and, as if he were looking for her, his expressive features creased in a warm smile. One graceful arm lifted to wave at her, and his actor's voice called out, "Peace, neighbor!"

Squinting against the brightness of the morning sun, Shelley responded to the casual greeting with a wave of her own. Her eyes followed his progress, studied his athletically lean body encased in snug jeans and a black sweater that clung to his torso like a second skin. She pictured him clad in eighteenth-century satins and brocades as befitted the hero-villain of her novel. He would be magnificent, she concluded.

Conscious of the direction her thoughts were taking, Shelley resolutely turned away. With purposeful strides, she walked to the desk, looked up Darby Webster's telephone number and dialed it. After a few rings, Darby's sleep-clogged voice came over the line.

"My God, woman, why are you calling so early?" Darby asked. "Has the plumbing given out?"

"Nothing has gone wrong," Shelley assured her. "At least, nothing mechanical."

"Good! Let me get a sip of coffee while you tell me why you're calling," Darby pleaded.

Carefully, Shelley related the arrival of the owner, posed a few blunt questions and received evasive responses that, with a little prodding, became informative comments.

"I take it you've met him, then?" Darby gushed.

"Oh, yes, indeed."

"What do you think of him? Isn't he unreal?"

"That about says it."

"Is he right for the part?"

"You knew he would be, didn't you?" Shelley asked. "You arranged for me to rent the cottage, knowing I'd eventually meet him." It was not a question but an accusation.

Darby chuckled. "Don't tell me I did something wrong!"

"It would have been nice if you'd told me straight out. I would have understood. The way it turned out, I'm a bit embarrassed."

"About what?"

"He didn't seem to know my name and I didn't really recognize his and . . . well, it got a bit sticky, especially when he started laying down rules for my conduct while I'm living in the cottage. He's a bit overwhelming, I must say."

Darby laughed. "You really like him. I can tell."

"I like his work," Shelley clarified. "I scanned his movies last night and he's very good. But I doubt that it's necessary to like him personally to enjoy his acting and know he'll do a good job in my film."

"No, I suppose not. It's just that I was sort of hoping you'd . . ." Darby sighed heavily. "You know, he's not married. Never has been. No affairs or scandals regarding women, nothing to besmirch that golden image of his. He's something of a renegade in the movie world, you might say."

"Or hasn't found anyone to love him as much as he loves himself," Shelley remarked dryly. "What does all that have to do with me? I hope you're not up to your old matchmaking games, because I'm not interested!"

"Oh-oh," Darby groaned. "So it's back to the Michigan farm girl with high ideals and the Garbo imitations. 'I vant to be alone,' is it? I should have known what would happen when you dropped out of the social whirl and got back to nature. Why am I surprised?"

"I do like being alone," Shelley said defensively. "Is that so wrong? Where I went wrong was in trying to be one of those aggressive modern women, flirting, pouring on the charm, being something I wasn't and wishing I could just be myself. Darby, do you realize that since I came here and things finally quieted down, I'm really discovering myself, who I am and what I really want out of life?"

"And who are you, Shelley? What is it you want?"

"I'm Shelley Tremayne, a product of the Midwest and proud of it. I'm well educated, and thanks to my education, I've been able to put a bad experience behind me and get on with my life, quietly, the way I've always wanted to. I'm a writer and a good one. I was a terrible news reporter because I had to struggle with shyness and scruples and things like that, and I was well on the way to truly messing up . . ."

Shelley grew quiet. Seeing a movement out of the corner of her eye, she turned her attention to the beach and gasped. David Warren was standing tall and proud in the morning sunlight, his bronzed body slowly revealing itself as he disrobed before her eyes. For a brief moment, she was certain he was totally naked; then she spied the light-colored swim trunks that concealed little from her view.

While she gazed in wide-eyed fascination, he leaped into the foaming water and began to swim with ease, his tanned body cutting through the waves with all the grace of an Olympic champion.

The ear-shattering sound of whistling captured her attention, and she realized that while Darby had been speaking, she had not been listening. Darby knew it, too, and had whistled into the telephone. It was a familiar ploy, one both women had frequently used when they had been sorority sisters at the University of Michigan.

"What is it, Shelley? Has your famous landlord made an appearance? Is he there now?" Darby asked in a hushed tone when Shelley at last responded.

"In the flesh," murmured Shelley.

"You mean, he's there with you and he's starkers?"

Before Shelley could reply, David rose from the water. With a predatory prowl, his firmly muscled legs carried him onto the beach, where his feet left deep imprints in the soft sand. His body glistened with beads of moisture as he lifted his face to receive the hot kiss of the sun.

"Yoo-hoo! Shelley!"

"I'm listening, Darby."

"Where is he? What's he doing? David Warren, I mean. Remember him?"

How could she forget him? "He's sunning himself on the beach. He just came out of the water like some pagan god," Shelley informed Darby.

"Is he that delicious?"

"Hm?"

"Honey, you're positively drooling, in case you didn't know. Your breath is . . . well, you know. I can feel your excitement over the phone, and I can almost see your farm-girl cheeks blushing red. Since you haven't reacted like that to any man since . . . well, in recent years, I can only assume that David Warren is even more spectacular in the flesh—your words, my dear—than he is on film. Now, tell the truth, is he stark naked?"

"He's wearing swim trunks."

"Oh," sighed Darby in obvious disappointment. "And you're there to see it all and blush prudishly!" Darby continued. "Now, me, I'm a red-blooded woman with natural desires and fantasies, and believe me, I'm fantasizing now."

Shelley merely grunted. She was unwilling to admit to her best friend that her own thoughts of David Warren were far from innocent. "Do you plan to visit me soon?" she asked, turning to a safer, more down-to-earth topic.

"You bet! I can't wait to see what the sun and sea have done for you. Shall I bring my collection of clippings on your famous actor?" Darby asked eagerly.

"You actually have a collection of clippings?"

"Well, you know how it is," Darby explained. "An important client who's a big star, a celebrity sex symbol . . . we all keep a file on our clients," she finished feebly.

"Okay. Bring your clippings when you come. When can I expect you?"

"I'll call before I come, in case you're in the middle of something . . . well, let's say something creative." Darby chortled.

"You're referring to my writing, of course," Shelley stated with good humor. "Believe me, you won't interrupt anything else around here. I've been ordered to keep my hands off the merchandise, if you get my meaning."

"What?"

"He warned me to stay out of his life, away from his house and his fiendish Doberman dogs," Shelley explained. "I agreed, of course, since I love this place and am hoping to finish that script within a few weeks. So much for your matchmaking hopes, Darby. Besides, I'm not about to get involved with another actor. You notice that I'm not off men, only actors. That's because I'm looking for true love, the kind that lasts a lifetime, like my mom and dad had. The only people actors can love are themselves."

"You are turning into a cynic, Shelley dear," Darby remarked.

After a few bantering comments, the conversation ended with Darby promising to call and arrange a visit soon. Shelley wandered through the cottage, drank cup after cup of strong black coffee and finally sat down at the desk. With her hands poised over the keys of the typewriter, she waited for her muse to make itself known. When she experienced nothing, she turned to the stack of neatly typed pages that was the first draft of the screenplay. Reading them over, she envisioned David Warren walking through the scenes, speaking the lines that were a direct translation from her book.

Laying aside the last page, she stared vacantly at the typewriter, awaiting a spark of literary inspiration.

Just when she was beginning to succumb to frustration, the telephone shrilled. Absently, she reached for the receiver.

"How's the script coming, Shelley?" boomed the exhuberant voice of Walter Elston.

"Right now, it isn't," she replied dully. "I'm blocked."

"No, you aren't." Walter, a leading literary agent and long-time friend of the Tremayne family, was always cheerful, Shelley reminded herself. "What's so hard about writing a script of your own novel?"

"Walter, I've never done a screenplay before."

"You never wrote a novel before you wrote your best seller," Walter reminded her gently.

"That was different," Shelley argued with her- self aloud. "I mean, the whole situation was different. . . . My motivation was compulsive then, I had something to prove to myself and . . ."

"And to Christopher Devon?" Walter finished with gentle humor.

"Um, maybe. At any rate, things were very different then."

Shelley didn't like being reminded of the un- derlying motivation of her novel or her reasons for writing it. Leave it to Walter to innocently bring up the painful subject.

"How much have you completed?" he asked.

"I'm about two-thirds of the way through, if you count all the things the movie moguls wanted deleted."

"Good. You're probably too anxious. Why don't you relax for a couple of days, forget the script and enjoy your surroundings? That cottage has a marvelous setting, in case you hadn't noticed."

"I've noticed," she remarked dryly. "Lately, the setting has gotten a little congested and murky."

"Oh?" asked Walter. "In what way?"

"I'm no longer alone."

For a moment, she was certain the line had gone dead. Then Walter laughed softly. "You've met him, then?" He didn't even say the name, she noticed. So, that's why he'd taken a hand in Darby's arrangements for the cottage rental.

"Um . . ."

"Is that a pleased 'um' or what?"

When Shelley offered no explanation, Walter cheerfully went on, his suave voice filtering into her ear over the telephone line. "Have you decided on someone to portray D'Arcy?"

"Of course I have."

"Anybody I know?"

"I've chosen David Warren," she said, pronouncing the name slowly and distinctly.

"Good choice. Have you spoken to him about it?" Walter asked, dispelling any last doubts that he knew Warren owned the Rehoboth Beach property.

"No. I'm leaving that sort of thing to you and the great powers who handle the contracts of superstars."

"I always knew you were a professional," Walter chortled. "How about the heroine? Any ideas?"

"Not yet," Shelley admitted with a sigh. "It's difficult to be totally impersonal when you're looking for someone to . . . to . . ."

"To portray yourself?"

"I'm glad not many people know that the story is my own," Shelley said grimly. "Think what the publicity people would do if they knew."

"It would make damned good hype for the movie, Shelley," Walter commented wistfully.

"Forget it! I bared my soul when I wrote the book, and you're one of the few who know it. I changed the names and the time period to protect the innocent—namely, me—and that's the way it's going to stand!" Shelley was adamant.

"My lips are sealed," Walter assured her. "The reason I called was to find out how you are and how the script is coming along. As for Warren, I'll start negotiating with his agent and see if a deal can be made. Meanwhile, you get yourself together, finish the script and mail it to me. Don't worry about the studio applying pressure. Remember, the agency still owns a large chunk of stock in the project," he reminded her gently. "The deadline can always be moved if things get too hairy."

Long after she had hung up, Shelley sat in a meditative daze. Unable to concentrate on the script, she found her thoughts drifting back to the traumatic months during which she had purged her heart and soul to produce a work of fiction that had taken the literary world by storm. Then back further, to the breakup with Chris Devon and its aftermath, to the time when she had withdrawn from her friends, forsaken the security of her family and ultimately given up a job that had been the envy of her associates.

After years of applying her talents on small tabloids, she had managed to move into the world of television news. Despite an inherent shyness and desire for the solitary life of a writer, Shelley's good looks and careful work had brought her to the attention of the head of a cable network. Financially, it was the offer of a lifetime, and once she had convinced herself to lay aside her literary ambitions, she found it comparatively easy to fool the public into believing she was a glib, outgoing television hostess whose interests ranged from the latest fad in cookery to chatting with the glittering stars of the entertainment world. Almost before she realized what was happening, Shelley had become a star herself, the smiling hostess of a syndicated television news and talk show headquartered in Boston. She masked her quiet personality behind a facade of bright patter and mannerisms acquired through a local acting coach, and the program's ratings continued to soar. Her fans were loyal and her future secure. It was an exciting time for Shelley, who continuously told herself that she was still young; there would be lots of time to write. After all, wasn't she doing most of the scripting for the show? And wasn't that a form of creative writing? Happiness, she reminded herself, was an elusive thing, enjoyed by few and unknown to the vast bulk of humanity. Success, on the other hand, was enviable and unquestionably hers.

Then Christopher Devon had come into her life and, after an exciting two years, proven unworthy of her love and trust. When the final realization dawned, it came with the force of lightning and left Shelley devastated, broken in spirit and more than a little intimidated by life itself. Feeling that there was nothing meaningful left for her, she had resigned her job. For a while she considered going home, but she feared that would be the ultimate expression of defeat. Unable to face the parents who had nurtured her and inspired her always to do her best, she used her substantial savings to travel. Soon, she discovered that she could supplement her income by writing freelance material that sold surprisingly well. Writing, she quickly learned, was an effective cure-all and a means of supporting herself without compromising her principles.

Then Walter Elston had suggested that she channel her abilities and use them to rid herself of any lingering feelings for Chris. Following Walter's sage advice, she had spent long agonizing months pouring all of her anger and passion onto paper. Somehow, her bitterness had become transformed into excitingly beautiful prose, which Elston viewed as having commercial possibilities. He persuaded Shelley to allow him to handle the work, and ultimately *Paradise Unending* had been published, receiving critical acclaim and overwhelming popular acceptance.

Shelley felt that she had not only accomplished her purpose of purging memories of false love, but that she had found something of value upon which to build a new life. It was the culmination of her childhood dreams, the answer to her avid prayers, the one thing above all others that she had always wanted, and life took on new meaning for Shelley. No longer did she have to pretend to a vibrancy that was feigned, or make excuses for her solitary lifestyle. Those who knew and loved her understood her needs and were pleased for her, happy that she had realized her potential, seen her dreams become reality.

But never in her wildest dreams could Shelley have foreseen the success she now enjoyed. There was no way she could have known that one day her private pain would be splashed across the large screens of theaters for the whole world to share. Nor could she have known that her literary talent would again take her into the glamorous world of actors like David Warren, who was, in his own way, more fascinating and perhaps more threatening than Chris Devon had ever been.

Chapter Three

Shelley stretched purposefully. She inserted a fresh sheet of paper into the typewriter, placed her hands on the keyboard and commenced to type.

Her fingers pounded the little keys; words appeared on the blank paper and soon she had completed a page of sparkling dialogue . . . and another . . . and another. Reading them over, she recognized that she had just written a whole scene that was faithful to the book she had written so long ago.

She worked until hunger pains growled in her stomach. Reluctantly leaving the cluttered desk, she absently threw together a small salad, which she consumed as she continued to draft the script.

It was dusk when she placed the fresh copy into a file folder, covered the typewriter and moved to the screened patio, where a gentle breeze lifted her hair and cooled her cheeks. Tilting her head forward, she massaged the tight muscles at the nape of her neck. Straightening, she fixed her eyes on the heaving waves crashing against the shore and allowed the sight to ease her tension and soothe her restless spirit.

When she returned to her unlighted living room, she slumped into a roomy chair and promptly drifted into the dreamless sleep of exhaustion.

When she awoke, she made her way to the shower. Ten minutes later, refreshed and tinglingly alive, she pulled a flowing silk robe about her nakedness and drifted out of the house and onto the beach.

An alabaster moon silvered the water, illuminated the shimmering sand. The night seemed alive with sound. Listening intently, she heard the familiar shush of the waves lapping against the shore, the faint echo of night creatures, frogs croaking, insects clicking . . . and the haunting, almost sensual strains of instrumental music. Casting her glance toward the main house, Shelley remembered the man who lived there and knew that it was his music she was hearing. But what music! A melody she had never before heard, its tone was majestic, captivating her imagination until she felt transported through time and space. The rhapsodic melody conjured hazy visions of mythical places peopled by gods and goddesses, nymphs and satyrs as it teased Shelley's senses.

Without conscious thought, Shelley's footsteps took her toward the imposing main house. Neither classical nor popular, the haunting theme poured over her like honeyed balm, beckoned her onward until she stood on a cobbled patio outside what appeared to be a library. Gazing through an unbroken expanse of glass, she spied David Warren sitting in a fireside chair, his head resting against its tall back, eyes closed as if in sleep. Anxiously she let her glance skim the cheerful room. The ever-present dogs were for once absent from their owner's side. Their absence was a relief to Shelley, who was unaware of making any sound until Warren's relaxed body tensed, his eyes opening to fix unblinkingly on the spot where she stood. Frowning, he rose and approached the sliding glass door. His fingers gripped the handle and thrust it open with an impatient gesture.

"What are you doing here?" he barked.

"I . . . uh . . . heard the music. I just wanted to listen. I'm sorry, I didn't mean to . . ."

His glance swept over her, missing nothing, not the drops of moisture clinging to her dark hair drawn back into a long braid that hung down her back, or the ridiculously trembling curves beneath the clinging silk gown.

"Well, now that you're here, come inside. You'll hear much better than out there," he said, his mellow voice seeming an extension of the rhapsodic melody filling the room as she stepped into the luxurious but spartan interior.

Soft lighting illuminated the room, which was a combination study and library with an open fireplace of fieldstone, comfortable but spare furnishings, a multitude of shelves crowded with books, and an uncluttered desk situated near the large undraped window facing onto the moonlit landscape. Everything was extremely tidy, Shelley noticed as her glance slid curiously over the room seeking the source of the music that had drawn her like a magnet.

"Are you familiar with this music?" asked Warren, his appreciative glance skimming over her from the top of her gleaming head to the shapely toes peeping out from her slippers.

"No." His caressing regard made Shelley painfully aware of her skimpy attire. She crossed her arms over her breasts, yearning to shield them from the heat of his eyes. "It's very interesting, though. Almost Oriental in theme," she added, wondering if his eyes had discerned that she wore nothing beneath the lightweight floor-length robe of floral silk. He would have to be blind, she realized, not to spy the tips of her taut nipples straining against the fabric.

"You're very perceptive," he declared, a touch of admiration underscoring his words. "This is something I picked up on a recent trip to the Far East. It isn't a well-known work outside of Japan or the Korean states."

"Oh? But it is well known there?" Shelley felt foolish, but she sensed that she was expected to say something halfway intelligent in response to his conversational comments. Her eyes moved constantly, resting on various parts of the room as if she were totally fascinated by the spartan decor instead of determinedly avoiding his burning eyes, which were studying her with obvious male interest.

"Yes. It's a form of folk music," he said, approaching her with a graceful but silent tread.

When he stood beside her, Shelley could feel the warmth exuded by his body, while her nostrils inhaled the clean scent of his maleness. "I'm familiar with the Orient and its music because I've done a lot of work there. The people are very friendly and always eager to share their culture with interested outsiders."

"You've been to the Orient?" she asked quietly, without turning her head. Her mental wheels were spinning as she realized that the movies she had enjoyed so much, set in the Far East, had actually been filmed on location. Should she continue to pretend ignorance of his celebrity status? she wondered.

His bemused laughter heightened Shelley's discomfort, and she moved aside to allow more space between their bodies. "Many times," he said in reply to her soft inquiry. "Are you wondering where the music is coming from? Look up there. See the speakers hung next to the ceiling? The main stereo is in another room, but the sound is sent to all the rooms from that center. I can enjoy the music anywhere in the house with this system." His hands closed about her shoulders. With surprising ease, he steered her to a comfortable chair and motioned for her to be seated. "This chair is perfectly situated for listening."

Shelley felt the coolness of his breath against her warm cheek as he leaned toward her, one elegant hand pointing out the speakers he had mentioned. His nearness was terribly exciting and disconcerting at the same time. For a man who so jealously savored his privacy, he seemed unduly anxious to please, she mused. Or else he was simply being a man, exercising his charm on an available female.

"How nice," she commented, her eyes avoiding his as she studied the rows of books lining the shelving that adorned one wall. "You can read and listen to music as long as the record or tape continues to play," she went on, babbling foolishly in her unreasonable nervousness. "You have a nice collection of books, too. classics, nonfiction, the latest best sellers . . ."

Shelley's words came to a stammering halt as her glance slid down the shelves to the narrow table beside the chair. On its smooth, uncluttered surface lay an obviously well-read copy of *Paradise Unending*. She leaned forward, and with a trembling hand she picked up the book to study its familiar cover. Her fingers riffled the pages and encountered slips of paper with scribbled notes written on them. Her eyes scanned the pages, scrutinized the marginal comments written in the same bold scrawl. It appeared that he had made an extensive study of the novel.

"Did you enjoy this book?" she asked with amazing calm.

"Yes, I did," he admitted readily. "It's not a particularly happy story despite its uplifting title. The book is filled with a great deal of tragedy and misery."

"It wasn't meant to be happy," she stated flatly, slamming the book shut and dropping it onto the table. It landed facedown and Shelley found herself gazing at her own black-and-white image on the back jacket. The photo, an old one with a decidedly serious expression, was not particularly flattering, but the publishing house felt it accurately depicted her serene features, her wide, slightly sad eyes fringed in thick lashes, her snub nose and unsmiling mouth.

Purposefully, she retrieved the book, holding it so that the photograph was beside her cheek before meeting David Warren's intently watchful eyes.

"You didn't recognize me or my name, I suppose?" she asked with a wry smile. "Yet you must have seen this picture every time you opened the book to make these voluminous notes."

If Shelley had hoped to embarrass him or take him by surprise, she failed miserably. He came toward her slowly, his unblinking gaze fixed on her face. When he stood over the chair, his hand snaked out, his fingers pried the book from her tense grasp and he studied the photo intently, darting curious glances at her from time to time as if making comparisons.

"It's not a very flattering photograph, is it? Doesn't show your freckles or that impish grin."

Shelley's nerves were at the breaking point. "Mr. Warren, let's not play silly games with each other. We're both adults. I know who you are and what you do for a living. It's obvious you know who I am and have known all along." Her tone was curt, her inflection pointed. "Since you've apparently made an extensive study of my book, you must know that innocence wasn't Lord Andrew D'Arcy's strong point."

Now he had the grace to appear slightly sheepish as he ducked his head and grinned. "I didn't immediately recognize you when we met on the beach. When you told me your name, I remembered that picture and told myself I'd have to introduce you to a good photographer, one who can capture your youthfulness and fragility," he said, his deep voice exuding charm and sincerity.

"Don't play games with me," Shelley said. "And don't think you'll distract me with compliments and flattery."

"It usually works," he murmured with a negligent shrug. At Shelley's exasperated grunt, he went on to say, "Actually, I'm surprised at your appearance. I'm also having difficulty believing that the wide-eyed freckle-faced sand urchin I'm now looking at has experienced all the tragedy and unhappiness that's in that book. I'd always heard that writers draw on their experience. Another theory shot to hell."

"But you admit you knew who I was all along! Why pretend you didn't?"

He smiled engagingly. "Not all along. I knew who Shelley Tremayne was, but you didn't look the way I thought Shelley Tremayne should look. You might have been her daughter, for all I knew, and when you didn't seem to recognize me, I'm afraid I decided to have some fun with you and let you think that to me you were just another summer visitor to this ocean paradise."

"And those ground rules?"

Ducking his head, he again smiled sheepishly. "Part of my joke. I didn't mean to offend you. It was supposed to be something we'd both be able to laugh about later, but maybe I overdid it a bit."

"Maybe you did."

"I'm really sorry. Forgive me?"

Shelley opened her mouth to speak, then closed it quickly. He was too quick for her, she realized, his sophistication, charm and disarming honesty quickly dousing the fiery spurt of anger that had flickered within her. As before, she had the sense of being bested, but she laughed and shrugged her shoulders in the age-old gesture of helplessness.

"You had nothing to do with the leasing arrangements?" She had to know.

"No. Of course, I looked at the lease and knew who my tenant was," he replied with charming candor.

"Then you came here to meet your tenant?"

"No. You see, I didn't get to see the lease until I got here." His reply seemed genuinely honest.

Shelley considered him in silence. Then, with a shake of her head, she said, "Maybe you're right. It might be that we'll be laughing later on, but it seems we've both been the victims of a bit of maneuvering by outsiders."

"Oh? In what way?" he asked innocently.

"You do know Darby Webster," she reminded him. "How about Walter Elston?"

"I only know Ms. Webster by reputation through her work at the rental agency. We've never actually met," he replied. "I don't recognize the other name. Honestly, I don't," he said with sincerity when Shelley's brows arched doubtfully. "Should I?"

"I suppose not, unless you travel in literary circles. Darby and I attended college together and became close friends. She knows everything there is to know about me. Walter is an old friend of the family. He's also my agent and business manager," she explained. "Both of them know who you are, even if you don't know them. Obviously, they arranged for us to meet. Fantastic as it sounds, there just isn't any other explanation for both of us being here at the same time, is there? I mean, you don't spend much time here, do you?"

Flashing a smile of considerable warmth and charm, Warren said, "I don't have much time to spend here. My work keeps me on the move. I've just returned from England, where I did a bit of Shakespeare at Stratford-on-Avon. When I leave here, I'm heading for California to talk about a movie deal with one of the studios."

"A movie?" echoed Shelley with a dash of feigned innocence as it occurred to her that the studio might be dealing behind her back. "Are you sworn to secrecy, or can you tell me about it?"

He flushed momentarily before lowering his eyes so that she could not read their expression. "It's still in the negotiating stages, but I've been told it's a screenplay adaption of a blockbuster best seller."

Shelley willed her features to a blank deadpan. "My novel was on the best-seller list and has been bought by a studio. And I believe it has been dubbed a blockbuster. But you won't be negotiating for that because the casting hasn't been done yet. I won the right to choose the actors and actresses for all the major roles." Her eyes were unnaturally bright as she met his interested glance. "But you already knew that, didn't you? I mean, you're aware that I'm in the process of writing the script and choosing the cast, aren't you?

"I'd heard rumors, but I wasn't sure," he mumbled, his customarily clear pronunciation muffled by something that Shelley interpreted as embarrassment at being found out. "So it's true?" he added.

"Yes, quite true."

"Most unusual," he pronounced. "How'd you manage it?"

"Very carefully," she quipped. "It's a long story, one I'm sure you're not interested in hearing. But we were talking about the coincidence of being here at the same time, weren't we? Do you agree with me that someone somewhere has been manipulating us? The studio, perhaps?"

Warren made no reply. His face was a mask of benign innocence. Shelley studied him, knowing that her interest was not only obvious but rude. Her eyes roamed over his broad shoulders, mentally measuring them before skipping to his tapered waistline, narrow hips and long muscled legs. Admiring the way his velour warm-up suit hung on his frame as if it had been custom designed for his well-toned body, she concluded that everything about him was impressive, even his silence. She yearned to discover a flaw in his perfection, but there was nothing immediately discernible.

It occurred to her that David Warren was not at all like Chris Devon. By now, Chris would have taken the initiative, charmed her by wit and meaningless words, left her breathlessly in awe of his superiority and cajoled her into offering him the prized role in the picture. Never would he have stood in relaxed silence, letting her examine him minutely, without saying something off-color or intimately suggestive. Of course, she could not deny the sensual tension filling the spacious room like a tangible presence, but somehow it was not the same sort of aura that had seemed to surround Chris Devon.

"About your book, Ms. Tremayne," Warren was saying, his words slicing through her wayward thoughts as if he, too, felt uncomfortable and longed to ease the tension that stretched between them. "May I ask a personal question?"

"That depends on how personal it is," Shelley said quickly, her nerves on edge for no particular reason. What sort of personal things was he about to ask? Had she been wrong in assuming that he was not like Chris? Chris would have long ago posed intimate inquiries, each heavily laced with sensual innuendo. "Everybody asks about the theme, where I came up with the idea, and so on," she remarked offhandedly, hoping to steer his curiosity in that safe direction.

"My questions are along the same lines," he replied, his glowing eyes holding hers as he eased himself into the chair opposite Shelley. "Naturally, the theme interests me. As an actor, I find it almost Grecian in its symbolism. Your Maryanne, so lovely, so gracious, so giving, reminds me of the love goddess Aphrodite, spurned by Hippolytus whose pride wouldn't let him love for fear of defilement."

Shelley laughed. Warming to his obvious interest, she asked, "Do you honestly see D'Arcy as fearful of defiling his body—or his soul, for that matter?"

"Yes, there's a thread of that in his character, as I see it."

He seemed so genuinely sincere that Shelley hastened to reassure him. "You're very perceptive. None of the critics found that. They saw the book as a sensational story of lust and misdirected love, revenge and ultimate death and destruction. That was never my intention. I had hoped to write a tale of pride and selfishness pitted against total unselfishness and true humility, the arrogance of D'Arcy versus the selflessness of Maryanne."

"Ah!" he sighed in satisfaction before posing other questions about the book and its many-faceted characters.

For hours that passed as mere minutes, they discussed Shelley's novel, delved into its underlying message and dissected the complex characterizations. Shelley found herself totally enraptured by David's knowledge, his understanding of what she had attempted to convey through a work that had begun as a psychological exercise and ended as a masterpiece of modern fiction. She could not remember when she had enjoyed herself so much, shared herself so freely. Not since Chris, who had never actually shown any interest in her work, although he had occasionally attempted to appear attentive.

Only when a meditative silence fell between them, broken by a striking clock announcing the hour of midnight, did they turn to each other and commence to laugh.

"I'm a very poor host, I fear," David said with an apologetic smile. "I offered you no refreshment and yet I've picked your brains with all the determination of a Lord D'Arcy. Is it too late to suggest coffee? Or something less stimulating?"

"No, thank you. I did promise not to annoy you, and then I heard the music and . . . and it stopped long ago," Shelley replied. "I must apologize for barging in on you and take my leave."

"Must you?" David sounded genuinely disappointed.

"Mr. Warren, it's very late. I have enjoyed our chat, but it's time I returned to my own little cottage. I'm working on the script of my novel and it's very taxing. It's my first screenplay," she confessed shyly.

"I'm sure it will be as successful as your novel," he assured her with a smile that warmed her heart and made her sharply aware of their intimate isolation. "I, too, enjoyed our chat. It was not only interesting, but greatly stimulating."

Shelley, not knowing exactly how to respond to his peculiarly phrased comment, turned to David with what she hoped was a gracious smile. "I'm so glad you enjoyed the book. You've certainly shown me that you understand what I was trying to say."

"Except for one thing," he said, rising to take her right hand in his. "I can't believe that you've lived long enough to experience the sort of thing you wrote about. It certainly destroys all my preconceived notions about writers."

"I'm twenty-eight, Mr. Warren, but I never said I'd experienced the things I wrote about." The strong fingers gripping hers were most disturbing and decidedly exciting. Quivering through her system was a sense of intimacy and warmth that made conventional conversation impossible, so that she found herself stammering.

"But you have, haven't you?" he asked, his fingers massaging her hand gently, tracing circles on the sensitive palm. "I can see it in your eyes. You may have reached the venerable age of twenty-eight," he mocked, "but you seem very young and innocent, untouched . . . until I look into your eyes. They're filled with pain and secrets." His free arm circled her waist, drawing her closer until their bodies touched intimately. Soft curves rested comfortably against hard muscles. His voice droned on, mesmerizing her. "Your eyes are so deep, they go down and down and down until I think I'm on the verge of seeing into your soul."

Shelley was unprepared for his whispered words, but her heart leaped into her throat and a delighted gasp escaped her lips.

"Really, Mr. Warren! There's no need to be so dramatic. I haven't forgotten that you're an actor, and a very good one." She laughed in an attempt at masking her secret delight in the touch of his hands on her body, the intense pleasure she felt on hearing his voice speaking so intimately to her.

"Make it David," he urged, drawing her closer into his searing embrace. "My name is David. Say it."

Shelley gazed at his sensual lips, studied them as they formed the quiet command. What would it be like to kiss those lips? Would it be a tender experience, or would it be devastating, earth shattering, heart stopping? Chris's lovemaking had been fierce, passionate and volatile. It had been such an agonizingly long time since she had been with a man, held in his arms . . . but her body remembered and made its own involuntary movements to mold itself to David's. Enveloped in the healthy scent of him, a blend of earthy masculinity and soap, she sighed contentedly.

David heard her sigh as an invitation, and his powerful arms drew her closer, his experienced hands caressed her lissome curves and brought her dormant senses to screaming life, suppressing all rational thought. Shelley lifted her face to his, her eyes gazing in trancelike fascination at the familiar features coming closer with each passing instant, the glowing eyes that seemed larger than life, the lips she yearned to taste. And why shouldn't she? This was no dream, no vain recollection of Christopher Devon. This man was real; he was here and Chris was but a distant memory, an almost forgotten ghost from her past.

Shelley's hands slipped up to his shoulders to clasp him tightly. Leaning into his solidity, she arched to meet his descending lips. Her thick lashes closed over her eyes as their mouths touched with an exploratory gentleness that deeply stirred Shelley's heightened senses and made her tremble with desire.

Hungrily, she allowed her passionate nature to surface. Her eager fingers moved through the lush thickness of his hair, caressed the chiseled jutting of his cheekbones. A soft moan came from her throat as she opened her lips to his seeking tongue. Eagerly, her tongue met his, welcomed its roughness and tantalized it in a fiery duel.

His head reared back momentarily as he gulped for air. Then, placing his lips to her throat, he licked gently at the pulse beating there. Exulting in the power she wielded over this virile man, Shelley molded herself to him once more, feeling the hardness of him pressing urgently against her trembling softness. His hands moved anxiously over the silk of her gown, seeking the velvet flesh beneath it. Cupping one throbbing breast, he kneaded it gently with his fingers, bringing the nipple into prominence so that he could toy with it through the fabric while his other hand searched desperately for a way beneath. When he at last discovered the secret, his fingers slid the zipper downward. The silky fabric drifted from her shoulders, landing somewhere about her middle as her aching breasts spilled eagerly into his waiting hands to be fondled until they were burning globes of raw sensitivity.

Stirred beyond sanity, Shelley murmured hoarsely, "Chris, oh, Chris . . ."

Abruptly, she was released. Weaving on trembling legs, she gazed drowsily into the dark face above her.

"Who the hell is Chris?"

The question was an outraged bark that crashed into Shelley's euphoric consciousness but at first made no real impression. Her hands still gripped him by the nape of the neck, pulling him back to her.

"My name is David." The remark was a hoarse cry, followed by a sharply indrawn breath. Gently but firmly, David disentangled Shelley's soft arms from his neck, leaving her wobbling awkwardly in her confusion.

"Oh!" she choked, collecting her shattered wits and gathering up the forgotten silk robe that hung about her waist. What had she done? Thoroughly consumed with self-disgust, Shelley clutched the robe around her still-trembling shoulders, whipped about, spied the sliding door and, after considerable effort, managed to slide it open.

Tears burned her eyes as she raced across the moonlit sand toward the dimly lighted cottage. Only when she was inside did she give vent to the frustrations licking at her like hungry tongues of fire. Throwing herself across the wide bed, she allowed her tears to flow unchecked. Sobs wracked her body, distorting the recriminatory words she hurled at herself far into the dark night.

Chapter Four

Shelley wept until she had no tears left. Even then, sleep eluded her as she lay staring vacantly into the blackness of night.

It was almost dawn when she remembered that David Warren had neither agreed nor disagreed with her about why they'd arrived together at Rehoboth Beach. She took his silence for assent at best, that they'd been thrown together on purpose. At worst, he was in collusion with the studio—which he would hardly admit.

Satisfied that she had discovered one devious flaw in David Warren's perfection, Shelley momentarily abandoned self-recrimination for going uninvited to Warren's house in the darkness of night. Turning her face to the tear-soaked pillow, she closed her eyes and made a concerted effort to sleep.

Her efforts were in vain for she could not

easily dismiss the exciting kisses of David Warren, the solidity of him, the scent of his maleness, the touch of his skin that still permeated her thoughts and lived in her memory. Adding to her emotional turmoil was the knowledge that she had thoroughly enjoyed those ecstatic moments in his arms, had been aroused by his caresses and been left unsatisfied simply because of her own mindless stupidity. Pounding her damp pillow with a balled fist, she scolded herself for having been so immature as to lose control of herself under the spell of such a magnetically attractive man.

Mentally retracing her steps, she recalled the mysterious music that had beckoned her to Warren's house. She had known that he was alone, terribly attractive and exceedingly desirable. Had she unconsciously desired to arouse his interest . . . his passions? Shelley was no naive youngster, unaware of her own attractions; she knew that men were drawn to her serenity, felt the need to pierce the wall of reserve with which she surrounded herself. Warren could be no different, she reasoned with a disgusted groan.

And yet I went! she agonized. Nearly naked and fresh from my shower, I actually went to him! He probably took me for a star-struck, sensation-seeking groupie!

Overcome with shame and repelled by the events that had transpired, Shelley tossed and turned. Longing for the impenetrable darkness of sleep, she fought the images flitting into her consciousness. Forcing her thoughts to fix on the work that must be done, she eventually won the battle with her charged emotions. Sleep closed over her mind, but it was fitful, and when she awoke she was still tired and lacking in energy. Surrounding her dry red eyes were blue-tinged puffs, mute reminders of the tears she had shed, the self-inflicted agony she had endured throughout the night.

Resolving to put David Warren from her thoughts, Shelley took her morning coffee to the desk and began to work. Soon she was immersed in the technicalities of her writing, absorbed in the characters she had created. So involved that the soft sound of footsteps crossing her screened patio made no impression upon her. It was only when she felt a presence in the room and heard a muffled cough that she spun about in the swivel chair to gaze blankly at the attractive man who had silently entered the house and now stood, tall and impressive, with his athletic frame etched against the bright backdrop of the sun-drenched beach.

"What are you doing here? Get out!" she ordered with an icy calm that belied the turmoil she was experiencing. Involuntarily, her anxious gaze swept the patio, half-expecting to see the faithful dogs following on their master's heels.

Correctly reading her darting glance, David laughed easily. "Fritz and Karl are basking in the sun in their pen, all safely fenced in and locked up."

Shelley let out a relieved sigh and then caught herself. Narrowing her eyes, she studied Warren in his faded jeans that hugged his narrow hips and thighs. Topping the worn denims was a knit shirt open at the throat to reveal the downy golden hairs of his chest. How dare he look so rested, so smug, so self-contained? Shelley fumed silently. Had the heart-stirring encounter that had left her drained emotionally and brimming with guilt meant nothing to him?

"I said get out!" she said again, hysteria creeping into her quiet voice. "You have no right to come here!"

His brows lifted quizzically. "Have you already forgotten that I own this cottage and the land it stands on?"

"I have forgotten nothing!" Shelley spat rudely. "It was you who said we were not to interfere with each other."

Flashing a devilish grin, he approached her. One long finger pointing meaningfully, he said with humorous charm, "But you broke that rule first. Now, it's my turn."

"You make it sound as if we're children scoring points off one another," Shelley remarked dryly, unable to look away from his attractive face. Their eyes met and held for long seconds while neither said a word.

David broke the tense stillness by saying, "Last night we discovered that neither of us is a child, so shall we abandon childish games?"

"Suits me." Shelley shrugged, reaching for her coffee mug to drain the last bitter drops that had settled to the bottom. "I would prefer that you didn't come here, but since you have, will you tell me why?" Unable to bear the heat of his intent gaze, she turned aside, setting the coffee mug onto the desk with hands that were visibly unsteady.

"I wanted to apologize for last night," he

began. "May I sit?" he asked, motioning toward a chair close by. At Shelley's nod, he eased his elegant body into the seat and crossed his long legs. "As I said, I would like to apologize for my boorish behavior."

With a restless motion of one hand, Shelley silenced him. "It is I who should apologize. I shouldn't have gone to you . . . your house," she corrected herself quickly. "At any rate, I did, and as for what happened . . . whether it was your fault or mine, it can't be changed by voicing a few meaningless words. It was nothing more than an affectionate exchange between two consenting adults," she said with an airy wave of one hand. "I suggest we accept it as such and forget it."

His sharp glance impaled her, penetrated to her very soul. "Do you think we can forget it?" he asked softly.

Shelley's heart leaped crazily. He had been touched by their shared caresses! she exulted. Aloud, she made an impatient sound. "Why are you actors always so dramatic?" she asked, mindful that there was always the chance that his sweetly phrased remark was nothing more than intentional flattery. "Are you programmed to be onstage all the time?"

"Are you acquainted with many actors?" he countered.

"I've met a few," she admitted ruefully. At his puzzled glance, she clarified the dry comment. "As you probably know, I used to be a news reporter. For a while I had a rather successful television talk show. In the course of my career,

I've interviewed many actors and actresses, even got to know some of them quite well. On the whole, they are a vain, conceited lot, consumed with their careers and advancing themselves." The moment the words passed her lips, Shelley regretted voicing them, for she spied the hurt that flickered darkly in David's eyes. "I mean, it always seems to me that theatrical people have difficulty touching base with ordinary folks," she stammered feebly, only to be halted by an uplifted hand.

"You're entitled to your opinion," he said graciously. "But I do wish you wouldn't lump us all together like so much damp clay." His protest was uttered in a cajoling tone that seemed designed to soothe Shelley's unreasonable bitterness. "Even actors are individuals with personalities that differ."

Shelley made no attempt to respond to his reprimand. She merely studied him, waiting for more of an explanation of his unexpected visit. Surely he had not come to take up where they had left off last night? she mused during what seemed a very long, tense period of silence that found them warily eyeing each other.

"Are you ill?" he asked at last, concern lacing the question.

"Why do you ask?" Shelley dropped her head self-consciously. With one hand, she swept a wayward strand of hair back from her forehead.

"You seem disturbed, nervous even. And your eyes—did you have difficulty sleeping last night?" he asked innocently.

Shelley's head jerked upward. Meeting his

bright gaze head on, she felt a nerve twitch in her jaw and realized that she had been clamping her teeth together tensely.

"My sleep habits are no concern of yours!" she snapped with unnecessary sharpness.

"True. I was merely concerned. Sorry."

"Stop saying you're sorry!" she snapped irritably. Why couldn't she accept his expressions of concern without wondering if it was all a carefully rehearsed act rather than an honest expression of interest in her well-being? "As a matter of fact, I didn't sleep well," she heard herself saying. "I . . . uh . . . had things on my mind. The script is giving me problems. I spent the night working out a particularly difficult scene," she fibbed.

"I see." His noncommittal comment managed to reveal his skepticism of her stammered explanation. "Is that the script?" he asked, his eyes darting to the file folder bulging with pages of dialogue.

"Yes."

"May I have a look at it?"

"No, you may not!" Realizing that she had once again spoken sharply, she smiled mischievously and said, "And don't even think of using your famous charm on me. The casting couch is closed for the season." Shelley was smugly pleased when he gaped at her momentarily before breaking into bemused laughter.

"You saw through me," he chuckled huskily. "I did hope to see the script, find out how you've handled D'Arcy and maybe determine my chances of nabbing the role. As for using my charm, well, forgive me for saying so, but it's a pleasure to exercise my charm on you, whether or not I get the part."

"You'll be contacted if you do," she stated. "You know how it goes—don't call me; someone will call you," she paraphrased, hoping to conceal the pleasure she experienced from his veiled compliment.

He made no comment. His eyes swept the room, coming to rest quizzically on the videocassettes stacked to one side of her paper-strewn desk. "I see you're a closet fan," he remarked with teasing grace. "Almost every movie I've ever made is there."

Shelley sighed. "I'm not actually a fan. Until two days ago, I'd never seen any of your films," she admitted. "And there were other movies besides yours that I've been looking at, so don't get all puffed up. Yours just happen to be on top at the moment," she said, unable to admit that she had already chosen him. Fixing him with an unblinking gaze, she said, "I'm beginning to think you are a devious man, David Warren. You set your goal and go after it, no matter what you have to do, don't you? The end justifies the means, I suppose, to men like you."

"I've never been forced to resort to the casting couch," he said with a slightly twisted smile. "I do admit to knowing what I want and going after it. That's good business sense and has nothing whatever to do with the acting profession, in case you didn't know. Seeing my work so prominently displayed does give me hope, though."

"Perhaps it is good business, but you actors seem addicted to leaping to false conclusions and building false hopes," Shelley remarked thoughtfully. "Everything in life seems to take on an aura of high drama for people who spend their lives in the world of make-believe. Even the simple sight of your old movies on my desk becomes heavily loaded with dramatic meaning."

Warren rose to hover over her, his eyes dark and unreadable. His expression was a curious mixture of anger and confusion. Unexpectedly, his right hand snaked out to cup Shelley's chin and lift it so that she was forced to meet his searching eyes.

"You either have a mental block on that subject or an axe to grind. I haven't figured out which. It's obvious that you're undergoing some sort of inner conflict about actors. Do you want to tell me about it?" he suggested in a mesmerizingly soft voice. "I'm willing to listen if you want to talk."

"Mr. Warren, in your continual search for drama, you look for situations that do not exist, that have never existed," she insisted.

"How quickly she forgets," he sighed. "My name is David."

"You're imagining things, David, fabricating your own truths."

"Is that what I'm doing?" he murmured, crouching before her so that their eyes were level. "Am I imagining things when I see hurt in your lovely dark eyes, hear pain in your voice, or read personal misery crying out from the pages of the novel you wrote?"

Unable to speak, to reply sensibly to his all-too-true suggestions, Shelley parted her lips. In an unwittingly tantalizing gesture, her tongue darted out to moisten their dryness. He was only guessing, she told herself, fishing for information, impressing her with his powers of perception in an attempt to win the part of Lord D'Arcy.

Before she realized what was happening, his mouth took hers in gentle possession, dispelled her fears and quickened her pulse. Tremulously, her hands reached up to cup his face in an effort to prolong the exquisite caress that was slowly deepening into passion. Her lips parted in invitation to his questing tongue, savored the sweet exchange, thirstily drank of his potent virility. With an unconscious motion, she twisted, molding herself to his needs.

When he fell to his knees, clasping her tightly to him, his hands gently massaged her back, Shelley moaned his name softly and allowed her fingers to explore the thickness of his hair, the rippling muscles of his shoulders, the narrow firmness of his waist. Her hands slipped downward over the worn jeans encasing his thighs, mutely cursing their very presence for interfering with her pleasure.

Abruptly, almost regretfully, David released her lips and murmured, "Sweet Shelley, you have known so little happiness. I can sense it. You're pleased to be with me, but afraid, and I think it's yourself you fear more than me. Don't deny it."

"I can't," she choked. "You're too quick for me."

"Tell me about it, Shelley," he coaxed between light, nibbling kisses that fired her senses anew. "Who was the real Lord D'Arcy? Was he an actor? Was his name Chris?"

Speechlessly, Shelley gazed into his face. How had he guessed? Was it something she had said or done? Was it her easy acceptance of his lovemaking that had betrayed her? The urgent mention of Chris's name at a time when she should have spoken David's? Surely he hadn't discovered her secret merely by reading her novel; she had so carefully masked the names, the situations, even historical periods.

Then she remembered Darby Webster and the slender thread connecting the real estate office with this dynamic man waiting patiently for her response. Despite his oh-so-sincere denials, Shelley was suddenly certain that David and Darby knew each other. At the very least, they had probably met and discussed Shelley's past at the time the lease was negotiated.

Freeing herself of David's warm embrace, Shelley rose and paced the floor restlessly. A multitude of conflicting emotions assailed her. She yearned to lash out, accuse David of having conspired behind her back; she wanted to scream, to give vent to the anguish repressed for too long, or, at the very least, to break something.

But she merely prowled back and forth across the parquet tiles of the floor, her bare feet soundless as she fought for control. Stabbing at her emotional stability was the almost overpowering need to speak freely to someone about Chris and what had happened between them, to purge herself of his memory and at last gain release from his unnatural control over her heart and mind. Why shouldn't that someone be David? It was possible that he was sincere, that he truly cared, that he actually knew nothing and wanted not only to know, but to help heal the gaping wound in her heart. Hadn't he already shown that he was a man of deep perception, able to decipher the hidden meanings in the poetic prose of her novel? Was it too much to believe that he had also perceived the motivation behind its writing?

Coming to a decision, Shelley halted her steps and turned her dark eyes to David, who still knelt on the floor in an attitude of patience and compassion.

"David, please tell me the truth," she said with amazing calm. "Have you discussed me with Darby Webster?" When he would have quickly uttered a denial, she raised her hand in caution. "I know you said you had never met Darby, but perhaps you talked on the telephone and she said something to you about me?"

His tanned face reddened visibly and his bright eyes betrayed his embarrassment. "She told me who you were and why you wanted to rent the cottage. She said you had been a successful newswoman who had turned to writing fiction. The novel was mentioned, and the movie deal. As I remember, she was quite enthusiastic about the script you were writing and went on and on about your intelligence and your fame, and I acted as if it was all news to me," he admitted.

"But did she tell you anything about me personally?"

"Nothing." There was no hesitation in his

answer. "For all I knew, you might have been an eccentric old woman," he added, his warm smile adding to the credibility of his comments.

"But you had seen my picture," she protested.

"Pictures can be altered. They are also deceiving and frequently outdated," he replied without a pause. "I hadn't yet met you, remember."

Shelley sighed resignedly. "I guess I have to accept what you're saying as the truth," she muttered, running her fingers through the tumbled curtain of thick sable hair that hung loosely about her tense face. "Are you sure you want to hear about me? About how I come to write *Paradise Unending?*" she asked. "I know you want to hear about Chris, so I won't ask."

At his assenting nod, she took a deep breath, stalked to the desk and opened the top drawer. Fumbling through the miscellaneous collection of pens and pencils, she found a crumpled pack of menthol cigarettes. With trembling fingers, she placed one between her lips, lighted it with the lighter snugged between the package and its protective plastic, and inhaled deeply.

"It's been a long time since I've even wanted to smoke," she said thoughtfully with a humorless laugh. "But then, it's been a long time since I've admitted that I was once the live-in playmate of an aspiring superstar. Believe it or not, there is a tie between nicotine and Chris Devon. Both are habit forming."

David smiled, his eyes never once wavering from her face as she began to speak of things she had never before shared with a stranger.

Chapter Five

Christopher Devon, a man of devastating attractiveness and unquestionable charm, had crashed into Shelley's life at a time when she was most vulnerable. Overwhelmed by the pressures of doing a daily news and talk show, the twenty-three-year-old Shelley was floundering like a fish out of water, attempting to keep step with the bright personalities surrounding her. Her social life, such as it was, had taken a backseat, but that didn't bother Shelley, whose idea of heaven was time to be alone, to meditate and plot her fantasies while walking in the woods or by a stream. Because of her work, though, the fantasies, too, had taken a backseat, and when she had the luxury of being alone, she drove to the country and spent hours reading the works of next week's interviewees, studying the lives of upcoming guests and writing the crisp scripts that kept the show's ratings high. Somehow, she managed to successfully suppress her need for a life of her own, coped with the stresses of her work and kept a bright smile pasted on her lips, but the strain had begun to take its toll by the time Christopher Devon came through Boston and was placed on the roster of personalities to be spotlighted on *Boston Alive*.

Vastly different from the men she knew, the crisp businessmen in their three-piece suits, the glib politicians who sought the favor of the news media, Devon's impact upon Shelley was lightning swift and soul shattering.

From their first off-camera meeting, the chemistry between Shelley and Chris was highly explosive. Their initial interview was filled with sensual implication and overt flirtation as each sought to plumb the depths of the other. To Shelley's chagrin and the absolute delight of the program director, this highly charged atmosphere was picked up by the camera during the interviews, which were stretched out over a week's time, causing the program's ratings to soar.

It seemed the most natural thing in the world for Shelley and Chris to become a twosome off-camera as well as on. Their first date was a mutually satisfying exploration of personalities, of passionate embraces and fiery kisses that led to Shelley's apartment where the affair began in an, uncontrollable blaze. Without question or regret, Shelley abandoned not only the bland men in her life, but most of her friends, in order to give herself exclusively to Chris. When he suggested that they live together, she agreed eagerly, forgoing the smart apartment she had furnished so proudly for the actor's Beacon Hill brownstone, a fashionable address suitable for commuting to New York, where he was appearing in a Broadway show.

"Everything was rosy until Chris was offered a part in one of those sci-fi spectaculars Hollywood does so well," Shelley explained to David. "It was only a small part, but the way he grabbed it, you'd have thought it was an Olympic gold medal. Positive he'd be the next superstar, he dashed to the West Coast."

"And you?" prodded David quietly. "Did you go with him?"

Shelley smiled dryly. "Of course not. My job kept me in Boston. And besides, Chris insisted that our relationship be our secret. Only a few close friends knew about us. Later on, I learned that it was *my* friends and not his who knew. I was young, and in love for the first time. Isn't that funny? A successful modern woman—or so everybody thought—thrown for a loop over a movie star, and a second-rate one at that!"

She took a deep breath, lit another cigarette and continued. "He made the film, signed up for another and got his name in all the gossip columns. He was photographed with hordes of beautiful women hanging on his arm, gazing adoringly into his eyes. There were publicity tours and trips cross-country. Oh, but he was faithful." She laughed grimly. "Called me longdistance, charmed me into believing he missed me and wished I were with him, strung me along . . . and I swallowed the bait like a starving fish even though I knew he was seeing other women."

"But you did eventually join him and share his success, didn't you?" David asked when she paused reflectively.

Tears smarted in Shelley's eyes as she shook her head in negation. "No. I was the faithful little whipping girl convinced I was the love of his life, the one he'd come back to one day. A year passed without him except for quick stops on his way here or there. When I seemed doubtful about our relationship, he'd use that charm of his to smooth things over and I'd find myself again waving farewell and awaiting the next fleeting interlude." Pounding her balled fist into the palm of her hand, she groaned, "How could I have been so stupid? I wasn't the gullible farm girl I'd been. I was a career woman, brainy and in the thick of things. Everywhere I turned, I saw hundreds of people just like Chris, saw them for what they were, but with him I—"

"How did you discover the truth?" David asked, compassion underscoring his words.

Shelley turned to face him, her eyes clouded with remembered hurt. "I wish I could tell you I simply came to my senses, but I'd be lying. I lived for him, waited for him, longed for him, never doubted him, no matter what I read or heard. Separations grew longer, but I told myself that only made our times together sweeter. We had a whole week together before he went to England to film a costume epic—another small part, but one that led to an Academy Award nomination. That week was pure heaven," she said wistfully. "Chris was like that, you see.

When we were together, he was so wonderful, so sweet, so loving. Before he left for London, he hinted at a permanent relationship for us and I spent my free time looking at brides' books and shopping for a trousseau like any starry-eyed kid. I took him at his word, assumed we'd marry when he returned, and live happily ever after. Do you know what I'm saying?" she asked David.

"This Chris sounds like the sort of man who promises heaven and delivers hell," David pronounced gravely. "And a lonely hell at that. The industry is riddled with men like him."

"You do understand!" Shelley said gratefully before returning to her narrative. "He came home from England, mouthing his customary sweetness and light. I asked him about the English woman he'd been seeing and he fluffed me off. I was persistent about that because I'd heard rumors and read reports that they were planning to marry. She was high on the British social ladder, so the affair was big news and, being in the news business, the item crossed my desk."

"How did he explain that?" David prompted softly.

"He tried to laugh it off, but when I showed him the news reports I'd saved from work, he stopped laughing and told me he'd met her while on location in the wilds of Scotland filming that costume picture. She was his ticket to fame and fortune. Well, at least to fortune," Shelley stated dryly. "You see, she's a distant relation to the royal family, a woman of power and means, a definite asset to an ambitious man like Chris. At any rate, he told me she could do more for him than I ever could, so he'd decided to marry her. Oh, he was very suave and charming as he outlined the future. His wife, being English and of royal blood, would live in England, so we could go on as before." Shelley paused, choking on her words.

Muttering an oath, David rose from the chair where he had been listening attentively to Shelley. "I don't want to hear any more," he insisted. His arms reached for her, gathered her close.

Offering no resistance to his soothing caresses, Shelley buried her tear-streaked face in the fragrant softness of his knit shirt. "There isn't much more to tell," she said with a forced laugh. "To make a long story short, I didn't handle things well at all. I told him off and tried to bury myself in my work, but everything fell apart around me. I never really liked being in the spotlight or being a television news interviewer, and besides, I was certain I was the laughingstock of the age, that everyone knew. . . . Everyone I worked with did know, you see. I was close to a breakdown when I resigned my job. Luckily I found some measure of contentment by venting my frustrations through writing."

"Why were you so devastated?" David asked. "It was only an affair you were well out of, wasn't it?"

Drawing back, she gazed up at him. "To most people, that's all it was, but I came from a loving family. My folks had instilled pride in me. I only wanted two things in life. Writing was one, and the other was a man of my own to share the good times and the bad. To me, falling in love meant marriage, a home and children. It would be forever, like it was for Mom and Dad. I guess it sounds corny and outdated by today's standards."

The tears flowed unchecked as she sobbed out the rest of her story. David listened, his hands moving comfortingly over her shoulders, his lips touching her forehead lightly, encouragingly. When she finished, he held her tightly, allowing her to release the pent-up angers and give vent to the heart-wrenching sorrow that had been too long held in check.

When she fell exhaustedly silent in his arms, he murmured, "It's over, Shelley. You wrote a damned good book, and the movie's sure to be a big hit." His hands gently shook her shoulders in a gesture of friendly affection.

Sniffing, Shelley tipped her head back to gaze up into his smiling face. "That's the sort of sweet talk Chris would have given me. Are you saying that just because you've found a part you want?"

"I can't deny I want the part of D'Arcy," he admitted. "The book was sensational and I'd like to be in the film. But I won't force your decision. Can you believe I understand and want to help you in any way I can?"

"I might," Shelley said with a halfhearted grin. "Try me."

He hugged her to him, murmuring, "How can I help?" Rocking her in his arms, he hummed softly in her ear as if that helped him to think. Finally, he tilted her chin up with his hand. "Are you having a rough time with the casting?"

Shelley nodded. "I've been out of the mainstream for a while, and I never have been a big movie fan. Mostly, I watch those old flicks on late-night TV."

"You're looking at a man who has friends in the film business and, if I do say so myself, I'm a good host for theatrical parties."

"Conceited brute!" Shelley said with good humor. "What's that going to do for me?"

"I'm not sure," he replied honestly. "I'm thinking of throwing a big party for you. I'll invite people who would do a good job in the film version of your book. You can meet them, talk with them and maybe make some decisions about the casting."

"Is this your way of softening me up so you'll be sure of being in the cast?" Shelley asked doubtfully.

"Of course." His honest reply was accompanied by a devilish grin. "What do you think?"

"It might be nice," she mused aloud, already considering what sort of people were among his close friends. "But, promise me one thing."

"What's that?" he asked, again folding her in his warmly protective embrace.

"Promise me that Christopher Devon won't be on the guest list," she said grimly. "I'm serious, David."

"No problem. I don't know Christopher Devon. And frankly, I'm glad I don't."

His voice had lowered to a threatening growl, and for some reason Shelley believed him. She snuggled closer to him, shuddering at the contained anger in his voice.

"You agree to the party, then?" he asked softly.

"Yes," she whispered into the hardness of his chest. "I can't wait to see this house come alive with a throng of people. It should be delightful."

Gripping her shoulders, he gently moved her away from him. When Shelley glanced up, she found herself hypnotized by his unblinking gaze, the unquestionable authority in the set of his features.

"Shelley, the party won't be held here. I have an apartment in New York, on Fifth Avenue. The party will be there. The sort of people I want to invite couldn't come here because most of them are actively performing on the Broadway stage or based in the city."

"New York?" Shelley echoed dumbly. "I don't think I want to go to the city . . . I can't!"

He shook her gently. "Why not?"

"Be-because . . . Chris is in New York! I mean, I read that he's appearing in a play off Broadway, but . . ."

"So? He may be in the city, but he won't be at the party."

"Oh, David, you don't understand!"

"Obviously. I was certain you said you were finished with him, that you haven't seen him for three years or so, and yet you're behaving like a nervous schoolgirl who has broken up with the star athlete and is worried sick about seeing him at the big game! Grow up, Shelley! If you were still doing that talk show, you couldn't refuse to face him, could you? Besides, New York is a big city and, big as my apartment is, it isn't large

enough for Christopher Devon." Pulling her
back into his arms, he pressed his lips lightly to
her forehead. "So what's your answer?"

Realizing how childish and immature she was
behaving, she lifted her face and whispered,
"Yes." Then, arching her body, she waited ex-
pectantly for his lips to take hers.

When they did, the sensation was sweetly
moving, the perfect antidote for the poison that
had consumed her mind while remembering
Chris. But when Shelley found herself snuggling closer in David's arms, wordlessly pleading for more of his gentle affection, he drew back
to smile into her drowsy eyes.

"Let's take a walk along the beach and plan
our party," he said quietly, his deep voice husky
with emotion. "I don't know about you, but I
need some fresh air."

Chapter Six

Shelley was fascinated with the bulging file of clippings Darby brought with her on her first visit, and the two women studied it with unconcealed excitement. Shelley wanted to learn more about David Warren, the puzzling man who had become a part of her life, and Darby was anxious to share her limited knowledge while gleaning more about the celebrated superstar who fired her imagination.

Unfortunately for both of them, voluminous as the clipping file was, it revealed little more than the customary publicity drivel, most of it fantastically unbelievable, that seemed to appeal to the public. There were numerous photos, a lot of speculation and many gushily phrased quotes from supposed friends and co-workers extolling the talent and personality of David Warren.

About the man himself, there was little information.

After she had scanned a few of the articles, Shelley turned to Darby and said, "Do you suppose he'll be canonized soon?"

Darby laughed. "He sounds too good to be true, doesn't he? The boss at the agency told me our client is a very private person, and it seems to be true. He doesn't do TV talk shows or give magazine interviews." She leaned forward, her expression intent as she lowered her voice to a conspiratorial whisper. "Now tell me what he's really like."

"You've never met him?" Shelley asked, wondering if David had told her the truth when he insisted he'd only spoken to her on the telephone.

"Never," Darby stated, adding, "But boy, that bedroom voice of his! Over the telephone, it's positively yummy! I came to see you mainly because I'm hoping you'll tell me all about him and maybe, just maybe, I'll get a glimpse of him!"

Shelley, who knew Darby's penchant for the dramatic and outrageous, pretended to be crushed. "And I thought you came just to see me!"

"Well, that too, but you can't blame me for being interested in a big star like David Warren, can you? Tell me everything you've learned about him," Darby coaxed.

Shelley did not immediately reply. Remembering the many pleasurable hours she had spent in David's company, she wondered how to answer

Darby's eager questions. She didn't want to reveal to her friend the nature of her encounters with Warren or relate the emotionally charged moments she had shared with the handsome actor.

Opting for a middle-of-the-road approach, she smiled and replied shyly, "He's a lot more gracious than I expected he'd be. When we first met, he seemed very intimidating and self-important. I'll never forget those rules he laid down, but then he told me he was only teasing—" She broke off, realizing that she had been about to say too much. Glancing away from Darby's intent face, she said, "He's planning a party to introduce me to movie people."

"You're kidding!" Darby seemed astounded.

"Would I kid about something like that?" Shelley asked. "Really, he's giving a party for me in New York and we're working on it together. He's handling the guest list since he's offered to bring me into contact with the right theater and film people."

"Imagine!" From the awed tone of Darby's voice, Shelley realized that her friend was dumbfounded. She couldn't remember when she had last seen Darby at a loss for words, and she secretly enjoyed being able to render the ebullient woman speechless.

"He wants to help me in making the casting decisions," she went on quietly. "I think he's making sure he gets the part of D'Arcy. In fact, he admitted it, but I still think it was nice of him to have a party. It'll be a nice relaxed way to meet some big names, don't you think?"

"Oh, sure, it'll be terrific," Darby agreed. "You have considered Warren for D'Arcy, haven't you?"

"I've not only considered him, I've chosen him," Shelley revealed with a gamin grin. "I just haven't told him. I told Walter, and he's working out the details. Those things take time, I guess, but I'm surprised David's agent hasn't already contacted him." Suddenly she paused and sat bolt upright. "You don't suppose he knows, do you?"

Darby seemed doubtful. "Would he go to the trouble of giving a party if he knew the part was his?"

"I don't know what he'd do," Shelley admitted, relaxing in the chair as her thoughts returned to the excitement of the past days spent in David's company, remembering his humorous insights into the people whose names were on his guest list, his apparent enthusiasm for the venture.

Only last evening, he had said, "If you can set aside your prejudices against actors, I'll bet you'll enjoy these people. Some of them are socially insufferable, but you forget that when you realize that they're geniuses in their own way."

They had gone over the guest list one by one. David offered his observations, some extremely amusing, of the idiosyncracies of the personalities he planned to invite, and Shelley had listened with the rapt attention of a child.

Her meetings with David had become very important to Shelley; his effortless charm and relaxed manner put her at ease, and she was looking forward to the coming gala. Through their blossoming friendship, she discovered within herself an openness, a willingness to make concessions for others that had been absent for a very long time. Not since her college days had she been able to put herself into someone else's hands and allow that someone to guide her. She had to remind herself that the relationship with David was a friendship and nothing more. Attractive and sensually vibrant as David was, Shelley could not forget that he was an actor and she was not about to allow herself to become involved with a man in that profession. Never again.

Still, Shelley was constantly aware of David, of his magnetic presence and powerful masculinity. And even though she could not tell Darby, a casual affection had developed between them. It was expressed through tender touches, searching glances and an occasional exchange of light kisses that sometimes deepened until they bordered on passion. Frequently she found their new closeness bewildering, but she could not deny that there was satisfaction and contentment in freely sharing not only her thoughts, but herself, with another human being.

"Darby, I'm not going to question David's motives," she said, surfacing to meet Darby's curious gaze. "I'm really enjoying myself. The party is a nice gesture and should be fun. I'm determined to enjoy it if I can."

"I'm glad," was her friend's sincere comment. "You look happier than I've seen you in ages. All this solitude and sea air agree with you. But then, you always were something of a loner, weren't you?"

"I guess so," Shelley admitted. "Since the big rush of publicity over the book died down and I came here, I'm a lot more relaxed and life seems worthwhile again. I guess I'll have to face up to the fact that I'm not the stuff modern women are made of. I still find the simple things, like solitude, good music and my writing, the most rewarding parts of life."

Darby smiled into Shelley's eyes. "I was afraid you'd discover how wonderful life here beside the ocean can be and give up parties completely, along with that glamorous career. I really envied you that job," she admitted. "But not what went with it. So I'm glad you're looking forward to this party. I wish I could be with you—for moral support, of course—but I'll settle for an introduction to the big man," she said, her eyes dancing merrily.

"I think that can be arranged," Shelley said, rising from the folding chair and motioning for Darby to accompany her to the beach, where David was walking his dogs.

As Fritz and Karl came to Shelley's side, eagerly leaping in response to her friendly greeting, David grinned warmly. "So you've mastered your fear of Dobermans," he said, his glance darting curiously to Darby, whose eyes were fixed intently on his tanned face.

"Just Fritz and Karl," Shelley qualified, patting each sleek black head in turn. "These two dogs have turned out to be absolute sweethearts." Pulling Darby forward, she said,

"David, I have a friend who'd like to meet you." She spoke quickly, hoping he would not be offended by her boldness. "I know you've talked to Darby Webster. Now it's time to meet the gal who handled the . . . ah . . . well, who arranged for me to rent the cottage," she finished, trusting that David would pick up her teasing reminder of Darby's conspiracy in the affair. "Darby Webster, David Warren," she said by way of introduction.

"Ms. Webster," he said pleasantly, extending his hand. "It's good to meet you at long last."

Darby gawked and stammered her way through a trite conversation that would later be embellished and exaggerated when related to her co-workers until it resembled a sparkling scene from one of David's movies.

"He's a doll!" she gushed to Shelley later when she bid her farewell. "I envy you living so close to him. Aren't you tempted to throw caution to the winds and let nature take its course?"

"Who's to say nature won't take its course regardless of my caution?" Shelley replied with an amused chuckle. "I mean, he's only a man, isn't he?"

"He sure is!" sighed Darby, her eyes closed ecstatically. "And you're only a woman. I wish I'd rented the cottage myself, but hindsight gets me nowhere." She got in her car and started the engine. "Take care of our superstar and feel free to do anything I would! That gives you a lot of leeway!"

When David left his beach house for the city to prepare his apartment for the party, Shelley came to realize how important he had become to her. Left alone, she frequently found herself feeling lost and out of sorts, anxious about the future and needing someone to talk with. At those times, she would make excuses to visit with Velma Anderson, David's housekeeper. Returning to her cottage, she would expend her energies on the script, working all day and well into the night so that when she finally sought the comfort of her bed, she readily succumbed to exhausted slumber.

After four days of solitude, loneliness and creative labor, the telephone rang. Eagerly, she spoke into the mouthpiece, hoping the caller was David. She was not disappointed.

"Everything's set!" he exclaimed, his deep voice warming her ear and sending thrills of pleasure through her. "Are you ready to face your adoring public?"

"Oh," she sighed, wishing his greeting could have been more personal.

"You don't sound very enthusiastic. Have you forgotten that this is your show?" When she made no response, he said dramatically, "Opening night approaches! Curtain going up at eight on Friday. Late arrivals will be seated during the intermission, which is timed for whenever their commitments allow them to arrive!"

Shelley laughed joyfully. His humor was infectious and she found herself asking, "No dress rehearsals?"

"Do you want one?"

"Isn't it customary?"

"Well, yes," he said with mock thoughtfulness. "All major productions have them, and this is a major production. Let's see, how about . . ." He paused. Shelley envisioned him checking an imaginary calendar, counting off the days. "This is Monday, and I'll bet you're knee-deep in an important scene of your screenplay. How about Thursday? Could you fly up Thursday afternoon?" His voice resumed its normal range as he continued. "I'll meet you at the airport, give you the dollar tour of Broadway. Then we could have dinner somewhere terribly chic before coming back to the apartment—"

"I'll be staying at your apartment?" Shelley interrupted. Her heart began to hammer against her ribs.

"It's a large apartment," he replied, and when Shelley said nothing, he asked quietly, "Don't tell me you'd prefer a hotel room?"

"It might be better," she said. "I wouldn't want to inconvenience you," she added hurriedly, aware that she sounded prudish. She hoped the breathless catch in her voice couldn't be heard over the telephone.

"If it were an inconvenience, I wouldn't have considered any of this," he remarked curtly. "We won't be sharing a room, if that's what's bothering you."

Shelley didn't want to admit to him that the thought had crossed her mind; it was, after all, exactly the sort of situation Chris Devon would have engineered, the perfect setup for a seduction. And why not? Hadn't she and David shared some rather physical moments? It seemed only natural that a man as virile as he . . .

"Shelley," he was saying, his voice deep and throbbing with sincerity, "we agreed that we're adults. Adults frequently share the same quarters without becoming emotionally involved. Don't you think we could survive one, maybe two nights under the same roof?"

Laughing at her own childishness, Shelley said, "I suppose we could. It's just that—"

"Just that I'm an actor and we've become close since that day we met on the beach," he finished for her, the teasing lilt once more lacing his vibrant voice. "You know I find you attractive, don't you? Am I supposed to apologize for that?"

"No, of course not!" She was quiet, sorting her thoughts. Finally she took a deep breath and let it out. "I think you're attractive too, David. But then, so do millions of women who don't know you." She laughed nervously and admitted, "I'm missing you, though. And I always thought heaven was being completely alone with my thoughts and my typewriter."

"You miss me?" he echoed, his voice warming her blood through the telephone lines. Unless it was Shelley's imagination, there was a happy lilt to the words that meant he missed her, too. But all he said was, "Then you'll be pleased that we're going to be together soon."

"Oh, I am," she assured him. Fearful of saying anything she might later regret, Shelley said briskly, "I'll hang up now. Got to make my plane reservation. When it's confirmed, I'll call you back. What's the number?"

She wrote it down as he gave it to her. Smiling

brightly, she said, "See you Thursday," and replaced the receiver in its cradle. She swiveled her chair slowly until she was gazing out dreamily over the tranquil Atlantic. In her heart, she knew the days until Thursday were going to drag out endlessly.

Chapter Seven

David hadn't exaggerated the spaciousness of his suite, Shelley discovered when she entered its elegant entryway. The eight rooms were a study in masculine beauty, outfitted with comfortable antiques that blended perfectly with modern leather furniture and glass occasional pieces. Everything was coordinated so that the colors soothed the eye. Wandering from room to room with David at her side, Shelley drank in the splendor of rich browns, greens and ochers that dominated the vast living quarters. In the luxurious bedrooms, tones of blue were accented by subtle off-white. The colors of nature, Shelley realized, expressing her delight aloud to the man who intently observed her reactions.

"Do you feel threatened?" he asked quietly, a bemused smile curving his lips.

"No," she replied honestly. "In fact, it's hard

to remember I'm in the city. This is so countri-
fied, so relaxed!" She was groping for the right
words to describe the quiet beauty of her surroundings. "This could as easily be a house
nestled in the woods somewhere. I love it! Oh,
David, it's so like you!" she said breathlessly, for
the apartment did seem to reflect David's personality, the graciousness that had come as
such a surprise to her.

He laughed quietly. "I was hoping for that
effect. My decorator will be ecstatic when I tell
her she succeeded." His bright eyes twinkled as
he directed her toward a room off the wide
hallway. "This will be your room. You should be
comfortable here."

Shelley drew in her breath, and her eyes widened as she gazed at the canopied four-poster
bed. Its embroidered hangings matched the tie-
back curtains at the spacious windows offering
a dazzling view of Central Park. The bureau and
chest of drawers were of antique rosewood,
which was polished until it glowed with a soft
patina and reflected the roseate hue of the thick
carpeting on the floor. A wing-back chair with
its own ottoman had been placed beside a small
desk that bore a few books and some small but
delicate carvings. "It's simply beautiful!" she
exclaimed.

"It's a room that seems to appeal to women,"
he commented.

Shelley turned to him with a quizzical frown.
"Have many women slept here?" The thought
was oddly disturbing.

"Jealous?" he countered, one brow lifting
comically.

"No, just curious," she mumbled.

"Ah, curious—but not jealous." He eyed her with a teasing glance. "Just in case there's a teeny bit of jealousy, I'll tell you that it was my mother who used this room for many years. My sister has also slept here. She refers to it as her room since she still visits me once in a while."

An underlying current of wistfulness in the remark caused Shelley to fix her gaze on his impassive features. "Your mother doesn't visit any longer?"

"My mother died several years ago," he replied quietly.

"Oh, I'm sorry to hear that," Shelley said with sincerity. It was apparent from the sorrowful mask that had settled over his face that David had been fond of his mother.

"She lived a good long life," he remarked, and his tone implied that he would say no more on the subject. "The closet is empty. Feel free to use it." His glance swung back to her, and he said, "I'm sure you're tired, so I'll leave you now. Oh, in case you're wondering, my room is at the far end of the suite. It's the other blue room, with all the books." His devilish smile returned. "If you call out in the night, I don't think I'd hear you from that distance."

Despite the bantering remark, there seemed to be an edge in his resonant voice. Shelley wondered if she had said or done something to anger or upset him.

"I'm not at all tired," she said, hoping to ease the tension stretching between them for no apparent reason.

Shelley realized that she didn't want him

to leave. The idea of parting was disturbing, though she didn't know why it should be. They had been together for hours, exceedingly pleasant hours of visiting museums, of strolling along the busy avenues of the city, laughing and talking, joking and rediscovering each other after their short separation. Every minute spent in David's company was exhilarating, she had discovered, and she was reluctant to bring it to an end.

"You should be worn out," he said, shaking his head in confusion. "I know *I'm* totally wiped out, and there are a lot of last-minute details that have to be taken care of."

"Oh! Don't let me keep you," Shelley said quietly, turning aside to study the books on the desk.

Soundlessly, he came to stand before her. His hand lifted to stroke her cheek. "I don't mean to sound abrupt," he said. "I'd love to spend a few more hours with you, talk as we did at Rehoboth Beach, but we have to be sensible about this arrangement, don't you agree?"

"I suppose you're right," she whispered, her hand covering his and holding it against her sensitive skin.

"Of course I'm right. If we're going to share this apartment tonight, tomorrow and possibly tomorrow night without . . ."

He broke off, and Shelley felt her heart dance crazily as she pondered what else he had been about to say.

"I really do have things to do," he said at last, his voice low and controlled. "Good night, Shelley." Dipping his head, he placed his lips lightly against her open mouth in a caress that was all too brief. "Don't worry about getting up early. My housekeeper comes in about nine, but I'll leave her a note asking her not to disturb you."

His warm breath fanned her fevered face. It appeared that he was having great difficulty maintaining his customary control as he released her, swiveled jerkily and walked from the room, soundlessly pulling the door closed behind him.

Shelley took a sweeping glance around the empty room. Laughing mirthlessly, she plopped into the wing-back chair and propped her feet on the ottoman, absently wiggling out of her high-heeled shoes.

You're asking for trouble, she told herself sternly. You thought he'd toss you on that bed and make love to you, didn't you? Suddenly she felt salty tears burning her eyes. You wanted him to do it! Don't you realize you're setting yourself up again? Walking right into it with your eyes wide open!

The party was an unquestionable success, Shelley acknowledged as she peered over the rim of her champagne glass into the crowded living room filled with the famous and near-famous. She was still trying to reconcile names to faces. There were so many beautiful faces, she mused. And a few not-so-pretty ones, like the round little man whose bald head was topped by an out-of-season suede beret worn at a rakish angle. A noted Italian cinematographer with numerous awards to his credit. Shelley had found him to be delightful, with a sense of humor exceeded only by his appetite for rich foods. Even though she had no control over such things, David had suggested that Vittorio was the perfect man to engineer the filming of the screenplay. The studio was already negotiating for his impressive talents, and David had invited him to the party so that Shelley could get to know him.

Then there were the wardrobe people David had introduced her to, the makeup artists who had studied her with narrowed eyes as if mentally reworking her pale freckled skin and fine features, and the assortment of technical people who were so important to a successful motion picture. The guest list was a cross-section of the entire industry, and it was enough to make Shelley's head swim.

And so many actors and actresses! Of all ages and sizes, with varying degrees of experience, and all endorsed by David Warren as worthy of her novel. To Shelley's surprise, there were a number of males who could qualify for the role of D'Arcy, each having his own particular appeal. She had not expected David to invite his competition and, because he had, she found herself gazing at him with unveiled admiration. Each time he came to her, introduced her to yet another possible Lord D'Arcy, Shelley's original choice was reaffirmed: David Warren was the actor she wanted and she would accept no other.

As the thought assailed her for the umpteenth time, she sipped her champagne and turned her eyes to his elegant physique. Studying the grace of his movements, the seemingly unfeigned warmth of his smile, hearing the resonance of his voice above the din of chatter, she asked herself if she was being truly honest with herself. Was her interest in him confined to his abilities as an actor . . . or was there a tinge of selfishness in her need to have him in the movie? A need to have him near her. To know him, be with him, enjoy his companionship and perhaps, in time, his love.

Shelley nearly choked on the bubbly wine as this last idea flickered into her consciousness. Her hand trembled as she set the glass aside and began to weave through the groups of theatrical people, her television talk-show smile automatically pasted on her lips.

"Shelley, dahling!" enthused a fortyish woman with gleaming bleached-blond hair piled high on her head, her manicured hand flailing the air as she approached. "Have I told you how I enjoyed your mah-va-lous book?"

"Yes, you have, Miss London," Shelley replied with a wide smile. The overly made-up actress had actually told Shelley this same thing about a dozen times. "I'm glad you liked it."

"Oh, but I did!" gushed Laura London, her broad British accent more pronounced than usual. "I was absolutely entranced with that woman . . . oh, what was her name?" Screwing up her face, Laura smiled excitedly as she pronounced, "Angelique! The one who cast all the spells and brewed all those weird concoctions. She was the one who really set the course of events, wasn't she, dahling?"

Shelley slanted a curious glance at the buxom blond, unable to believe that this aging painted doll envisioned herself as the filth-encrusted hermitess responsible for the sadistic character of Lord Andrew D'Arcy. Still, she *was* an actress, Shelley reasoned, knowing a sense of admiration for the woman's ability to discern the subtleties of the characterization. Despite her flibbertigibbet off-screen mannerisms, Laura undoubtedly was knowledgeable about her craft.

"Angelique was D'Arcy's mother," Shelley said in reply to Laura's question. "The seeds she planted in the child bore bitter fruit in the adult D'Arcy."

"That's the way I saw it!" Laura's plump hand rested on Shelley's shoulder. "I do hope Angelique's part isn't cut in the film version. It wouldn't be fair to the audience, would it?"

"It isn't being cut," Shelley assured her.

Laura seemed to relax, but her hold on Shelley tightened possessively. "Davey told me you're writing the script. I find that fascinating, dahling! Just fascinating!"

"Davey?" Shelley smothered a giggle. She couldn't picture David Warren with that nickname. It conjured visions of golden-haired choirboys and stammering youths. "You mean David Warren," she said, her expression bland. "He probably also mentioned that I've got a hand in the casting decisions."

"Yes, but that's incredible! Most unusual," murmured Laura, who was eyeing her curiously as she steered her into an unoccupied corner where she dropped to a settee in a flounce of lavender organza. "Don't you think Davey's perfect for D'Arcy?" she whispered confidentially. "I mean, he's so handsome on the surface and so rotten underneath." Her rippling laughter rang out. "D'Arcy, I mean, not Davey! Davey's good through and through."

"You really like him, don't you?" Shelley asked, succumbing to the older woman's verbosity.

Laura sighed, and her bright eyes twinkled mischievously as they searched the room until she spied David. "He reminds me of my fifth husband."

"Your fifth . . . ?" Shelley wanted to laugh but was uncertain whether or not the actress was joking. "How many husbands have you had, Miss London?" she asked.

"Only four," Laura sighed with a wink at her own joke. "Forgive me. I began in vaudeville, and my first real theater experience was as a stand-up comedienne. Once in a while, I revert back."

Shelley turned aside, laughter bubbling in her throat. Her amused glance locked onto David's seeking eyes, and she sent a message that he correctly interpreted, hastening to her side.

"Shelley, I think I've found the perfect Maryanne," he said. "Come and meet her." With a devastating smile slanted at Laura, he apologized profusely for interrupting their conversation. He placed his hand beneath Shelley's elbow, and directed her to a group of young people.

"Have you really found a Maryanne?" Shelley asked as he propelled her ahead of him.

"I think so, but I got the impression you'd had enough of Madam London," he murmured, bending to speak into her ear.

"Too right. Would you believe she's determined to play Angelique?"

David halted his steps to consider Shelley for a moment. His eyes darted to Laura's gleaming blond head, and he seemed to be seeing something that was invisible to Shelley. "Not a bad idea," he said reflectively. "Laura's a terrific actress."

"But Angelique?" Shelley protested.

"You take too much at face value," he said with a chuckle. "Makeup artists can take a face like Laura's and, before your very eyes, *voilà!* Angelique!"

As she mulled over the possibility, Shelley allowed David to introduce her to several young actors and actresses whose names made no immediate impression because of their youth and lack of exposure.

"Are you planning to write another book, Ms. Tremayne?" asked an attractive young woman with reddish brown hair and a complexion of cream.

"Sooner or later, I hope to start another. I have to prove the first one wasn't a fluke!" Shelley replied. "Right now, I'm tied up with the screenplay. I haven't the time to consider new plots and develop characters."

"You'll hear more from Shelley one day, Jenny," David assured the girl, whose large dark eyes rested unblinkingly on his smiling face. "She'll be the next Charlotte Brontë."

"Oh, I'm sure she will," said the girl. "You're so young, Ms. Tremayne!" she said to Shelley with a touch of shyness. "I expected the author of *Paradise Unending* to be at least fifty."

Embarrassed by the girl's open admiration, Shelley merely smiled. David's fingers gripped her upper arm, his thumb moving in caressing circles over the flesh and causing her nerve ends to tingle alarmingly.

"I realize Jenny's very young," he said in a voice intended only for Shelley's ears. "She's got good experience, though. She's done wonderful work in summer stock and community theater. I'm sure she'd do a good job as Maryanne."

Shelley murmured an acknowledgment of his comments and flashed Jenny a smile. "So, you've read the book. Did you like it?"

"Yes." The girl's eyes moved quickly from Shelley to David and back again. "It was so nice of you both to invite me to the party. I've enjoyed it."

"It was our pleasure," David replied. "Don't leave yet. The evening is young. But we have to move on and circulate so nobody feels slighted."

"The child has a crush on you," Shelley informed David hours later when the last of the guests had departed and they sat in companionable exhaustion, quietly going over the high points of the evening. Their voices were low, almost hushed, as they sat close together on the leather sofa in David's study, where the last remnants of a once blazing fire flickered in the intimate darkness of the room.

"Who?" he asked.

"Young Jenny Sinclair, the one who was so surprised that I'm not a middle-aged frump. I thought she was a wee bit jealous of me. Of us, I should say."

Without lifting his head resting against the

smooth leather, David shot a questioning glance at Shelley. "Why would Jenny envy us?"

"You tell me," Shelley replied. "I just met her tonight. You've known her for a while, haven't you?"

"We worked together a few years ago when she was starting out," he admitted thoughtfully. "As I recall, she was properly respectful of my superior talents," he added with mock conceit. "I didn't know she was smitten. It takes a woman to notice things like that. Care to tell me what you think of her for Maryanne, or are you too envious of her youth and infatuation with me to be objective?"

"I'm not envious of her," Shelley insisted without conviction. "I'm too tired to consider anybody for anything tonight, David." In all honesty, it wasn't weariness or envy that caused her to evade David's question. She simply wanted nothing to intrude upon their private moment.

David's hand reached for hers, clasped it and held it tightly. His thumb traced sensual circles on her palm. "But you enjoyed yourself tonight, didn't you?"

"Immensely," Shelley replied. "You were right when you said you're good at hosting parties, but I marvel at how you cope with all those emotional theater people." She was glad that the talk of jealousy had been left behind. All she wanted was to enjoy the exciting touch of his fingers, the warmth they communicated to her.

"You didn't do so bad yourself," he murmured, leaning forward to press his lips lightly against her cheek. "I was proud of you. I doubt anyone suspected that you had reservations about this sort of thing. You were not only gracious, you looked—correction, look—absolutely smashing. You should always dress in red."

Shelley glanced at him from the corner of her eye while her fingers smoothed the folds of the cranberry caftan that was one of her favorite evening outfits. Of flowing silk, loosely fitted, it allowed freedom of movement while giving the impression of regal elegance. Red was her favorite color; it gave her courage. And she had deliberately kept the gown's clean lines uncluttered by wearing only a heavy gold medallion around her neck with matching earrings. "I didn't think you noticed," she murmured.

"I noticed. I notice everything about you," he whispered hoarsely, his lips only inches from hers. "The way you walk, the breathless intonation of your voice, the little flame that dances in your eyes when you're pleased as you are now . . ." His mouth hovered over hers, his words whispered into her slightly parted lips.

Turning toward him, she placed her hands on his shoulders and felt the solidness of him beneath her questing fingers. "That sounds like a bit of dialogue from an old movie," she said, attempting to still the restless beating of her pulse.

"It's late, my darling," he murmured against her lips, the touch of his mouth stirring her more than an actual kiss could have done. "We're alone, bathed in the afterglow of a successful evening. Forgive a humble actor for being slightly dramatic, but I'm tired and happy and susceptible."

His free hand moved, caressing her body with fingers of fire, awakening it to its potential as his hand roamed freely over her hips, up to her small waist, across her rib cage to the underside of her unfettered breasts. Shelley made herself available to him, sighed her pleasure when his hand cupped her left breast, the thumb teasing the nipple to taut erectness. Forgotten were all her doubts and reservations where this man was concerned. Now she eagerly accepted his intimate overtures, welcoming and encouraging each provocative gesture.

Nibbling at her lower lip, he moaned softly, and she eagerly smothered the sound with her mouth so that she could taste his special flavor.

His hands moved hungrily over the lush silk of her gown while his lips slid over her face and throat, planting softly tantalizing kisses along the way.

Again he groaned as she arched against him in search of a more complete closeness. "My God, Shelley!"

"Yes?"

When there was no reply to her husky whisper, she knew that he was as immersed in the pleasurable moment as she. The increasingly urgent explorations of his hands delighted her, and she began her own inventory of his magnificent body. Overcome with emotion, she allowed her hand to roam his chest at will with stroking movements that brought agonized groans from deep within his throat.

"Shall we go to the bedroom?" he rasped as his hands fumbled with the fabric of her dress.

"Don't stop, David!" she sighed, molding her

body to his so that his hands had free access to the curves of her back. When his fingers closed over the zipper fastening and slid it down, freeing her heated flesh to the coolness of the room, she purred like a kitten and shrugged out of the whispering silk. Extending her arms toward him, she murmured, "You've got too many clothes on. Let me help."

With fingers that were amazingly steady, she slid his elegant evening jacket from his shoulders and let it drop to the floor. Then she turned her attention to the small pearl buttons of his silk shirt, undoing them quickly and thrusting the garment aside. Her fingers splayed over the soft mat of hair on his chest, paused to savor the beat of his heart and then continued to explore.

David's mouth moved over her, first on her open lips, then downward to her throat, collarbone, down still further until they closed over one throbbing nipple. His tongue laved the tip, then left it aching for still more as he sought the other breast, suckled it with the same thoroughness, tongued it into a sensitive peak of redness and then moved on to taste the sweetness of her naked belly and thighs.

Aquiver with desire, Shelley sought to bring the sweet agony to completion. Her fingers moved urgently over him, stroking his firm buttocks and pleading for a speedy joining.

But David seemed in no hurry. His movements were slow, calculated and deeply, erotically exciting.

Their eager bodies clung like matched pieces of a puzzle, straining for the ultimate closeness. Together their entwined bodies slid from the settee to the floor. Shelley landed on top and, chuckling gleefully, she pressed herself urgently to his masculinity. Her feverish tongue licked at his nipples, brought hungry cries from his lips and urgency to his movements. When her tongue darted downward over the taut muscles of his stomach and lower still, he grasped her by the shoulders and held her off.

"Now, Shelley?" he asked, his voice a choked cry. "Here?"

"Now!" she responded, allowing him to lift her into place, to fill her with his throbbing masculinity, and together they embarked on a gasping journey through the rapturous realm of physical pleasure.

Their coming together was at once violent and unbelievably gentle as they rocked back and forth, swirled round and round, rose and plunged through the steps of an intricate dance that was as old as time itself. Wanting to prolong their mutual pleasure, each sought to match the other's rhythm, but when the voluptuous summit of gratification was reached, it came with the force of a thunderbolt. Unable to sustain the precious rapture, they crashed through the mystical veil of sensation and plummeted back into the reality of the night.

Clasped in each other's arms, they closed their eyes, gulped for air and waited for the rapid beating of their two hearts to slow. Few words had been spoken; the only sounds had been sighs and ecstatic gasps, but it didn't seem to matter for there was no need for conversation. Their two bodies had spoken eloquently and well.

Chapter Eight

Shelley slept and dreamed of David Warren, who held her in loving arms, caressed her, kissed her eager lips with sweet passion and brought her body into sensual awareness. The visions that crept into her drowsing consciousness took on an aura of reality, so that when her dream lover lifted her in powerful arms and moved with sure steps down a long dark hall, she struggled to awaken. But the blissful fantasy held her enthralled and she slept on.

Soft words cascaded over her, comforted her and aroused all her sleeping senses. Stirring, she snuggled closer to the naked male body, warm and familiar, lying beside her. Sighing contentedly, she savored the healthy male scent enveloping her like a cloud and settled to rest her weary body and mind.

Only when she felt the feathery touch of warm

lips circling her own, tantalizing them and bringing her to full wakefulness, did her eyelids flutter open. Gazing uncomprehendingly into the face hovering above her, she did not immediately recognize the man whose glowing eyes shone in the shadowy darkness. But when he smiled, revealing twin dimples, she knew it was David and her heart rejoiced.

Returning the smile, her eyes slid from his to the dimness beyond his broad bare shoulder. A small frown creased her brow as she beheld the golden glow of lamplight illuminating blue walls lined with shelving. Rising up on her elbows, she peered at the elegantly masculine furnishings.

"This is your room?" she whispered.

"Yes."

"How did I get here?"

"How do you think? I brought you, sleepyhead. You were out like a light. Too much champagne or too much . . . ah . . . physical activity?" he asked with teasing lightness.

The dream returned to Shelley's drowsy consciousness and she realized that it had been no dream. The arms carrying her had been real. Had the lips that had fired her senses been real as well, or a part of some ecstatic half-dream?

When she would have posed the questions darting anxiously through her groggy mind, David lowered himself until he was beside her, propped up on one elbow. His delightfully passion-glazed eyes gazed deeply into hers, held them and dared her to deny the sensuality that existed between them.

"Shelley, don't talk. It isn't necessary."

His husky murmur infiltrated her brain, shot through her nervous system and warmed it like liquid fire. "We can talk later."

Accepting his words, Shelley nodded, then lifted her face for his cupping palm. When his lips lightly traced hers, she sighed. Opening her mouth, she welcomed the invasion of his rough tongue, met it with her own and felt desire igniting in the very core of her being. Her slender arms circled his shoulders; her body molded itself to his. Savoring the touch of flesh against flesh, her hips began to writhe restlessly beneath his experienced hands that were now well acquainted with her most responsive places.

When his fingers found the highly sensitive flesh on the inner side of her thighs, she moaned his name, parted her legs and clutched him to her, inviting his sweet penetration.

This time, they came together with a flaming intensity that defied sanity, swept them along on a raging tide of emotion that was at once consuming and shared. Crying out their mutual joy in one another, they soared as one to the summit of ecstasy, paused there to inhale the rarefied glory of oneness, and then plunged headlong into pure sensation as the universe seemed to explode into shards of blazing light, too glaring to last, too sweet to be quickly forgotten.

It was nearly daybreak when Shelley finally stirred, her extended arm searching for David's muscular warmth. When she encountered nothing but satin-soft sheets and a crumpled pillow, she was not alarmed. Burying her face in the fragrant pillow, she breathed in the scent that was peculiarly David's and knew a sense of completion and tranquillity.

When she heard muffled sounds beyond the closed door of the bedroom, she stretched and rose from the warm bed to discover that she was naked, with nothing to cloak her. Spying a closet, she moved toward it, slid the door soundlessly along its track and studied the many masculine outfits.

Selecting a terry robe that hung to her ankles, she tied it about her and cautiously entered the sunlit passageway that led to the main living quarters.

"Good morning, miss."

The crisp female voice caught Shelley off guard, and she clutched the robe about her. "Good morning," she answered, her voice slightly stilted as she studied the middle-aged, plump and ruddy-complected woman who stood before her. The dustcloth in her hand told Shelley that this was the woman who cared for David's apartment. No doubt she had seen many women as scantily clad as Shelley, but somehow that knowledge brought no comfort.

"Mr. Warren said not to disturb you," the housekeeper was saying apologetically. "I hope I didn't make too much noise."

"No, it's time I got up," Shelley remarked, then asked, "What time is it?"

"Almost noon," was the easy response. "Mr. Warren had to go out, but he said to tell you there's food in the kitchen and to make yourself at home."

"Oh. Thank you. Which way is the kitchen?" Shelley asked, unable to remember the layout of the suite.

The housekeeper's smile widened as she led the way to a sparkling kitchen that had the immaculate appearance of disuse. Standing in the arched doorway, Shelley found it difficult to believe that a lively party had been run out of this spartan room the night before.

"Thank you," she said to the housekeeper, who beamed at her from a respectful distance. "I can't keep saying 'you' all the time. What's your name?"

"I'm Millie Rogers. Mr. Warren calls me Millie. Can I fix something for you?"

"No, but thank you, Millie. You go ahead and make all the noise you like," Shelley assured her with a smile. "I'll be leaving soon. All I want is some juice and a quick shower." She hoped she sounded appropriately casual, but sensed that her bravado fell short as she opened the door of the refrigerator.

"Mr. Warren should be back soon. He seemed to think you'd be waiting for him," Millie said. "Oh, I sent a beautiful red silk gown to the cleaners to be pressed. Would that be yours?"

"I'm afraid so," Shelley replied, sipping a tumbler of grapefruit juice. "But don't worry, I have other clothes." She laughed. "Well, I guess if Mr. Warren expects me to wait for him, I'd better take that shower, get dressed and make a couple of phone calls. I don't think he'd mind." Her words were not intended for Millie, but were the mere voicing of her thoughts. "Oh, don't mind me," she said quickly, realizing that she had confused the housekeeper by sounding as if she were asking her permission. "I'm just a bit groggy from the party. I'm thinking out loud."

With a last quizzical glance, Millie turned away. As Shelley entered the luxurious bath, with its satin and tufted appointments, she heard the hum of a vacuum cleaner.

Since David had not returned by the time Shelley had showered, dressed in a fashionable, man-tailored silk pantsuit, and carefully applied makeup to her freckled face, she telephoned Walter Elston to let him know she was in town. He asked her to drop by his office and promised to make time for her.

"I don't have much time, Walter," she explained doubtfully. "I have a plane reservation for six this evening. I only called to find out if there have been any developments in the movie deal and to tell you the script should be in your hands within two weeks."

"Terrific. And since I have papers for you to sign and news to relate, why don't you stop in this afternoon on your way to the airport." He waited for her to agree before adding, "I have good news, really good news, for you."

"And what is that?"

"Your friend has agreed to do the film. From what I've heard, he was simply waiting for a bid." Walter chortled merrily. "I got the impression he'd have done it for free, or for a mere pittance. He wanted that part so bad, he'd have accepted anything offered to him."

"Are we talking about David Warren?" Shelley asked, trying to comprehend Walter's words. Her throat seemed unduly tight, and a shiver of coldness spiraled up her spine.

"Didn't you say he's the friend you're visiting?" Walter sounded slightly impatient. "I thought you two had become quite close, at least close enough to talk about this deal. In talking to his manager, I got the impression that Warren was pleased as punch with his success in winning you over. His manager was pretty cocky about the whole thing. As I recall, the expression he used was, 'Tremayne is a tough nut to crack.'"

"Winning me over?" Shelley echoed numbly. "Did David actually say I'm a tough nut to crack?"

"I haven't spoken with Warren, Shelley, love. His manager told me the great star said words to that effect."

"Then he probably did say it," Shelley mused aloud. Shuddering, she forced brightness into her voice as she assured Walter she would meet him at his office later.

Shelley dropped the receiver onto its cradle and began to pace the carpeted floor of the study. Muttering angry recriminations, she chided herself for once again being susceptible to the dubious charm of an actor, for allowing herself to be made a fool of and for falling under the spell of a man who ruthlessly used his dramatic skills to win her trust and confidence. Hadn't she learned her lesson with Chris? Was she so desperate for male affection that she had turned a deaf ear and blind eye to the warnings she had given herself? Of course, she reminded herself grimly, David's methods were slightly different. Each time she had confronted him on a small point, he had given her an honest answer and that beguiling smile, and she had accepted his replies. Deceiving through honesty, she mused, was a new trick, one she would remember the next time.

The rapturous lovemaking of the previous night took on an aura of shabbiness, became sordid in her imagination. Now, she feared that the interlude had been nothing more than David's selfish means of expressing gratitude, or perhaps even assuring that she would not change her mind; he had, after all, invited his competition to the party, hadn't he?

In retrospect, what had seemed to Shelley to be a truly beautiful experience became, in reality, a calculated seduction for the sole purpose of furthering David Warren's career. And she must accept it for what it was.

Pounding her balled fist against the leather surface of the sofa where she had succumbed to David's persuasive attractions, Shelley cursed the man who had taken her along the path to false paradise.

Coming to a decision, she squared her shoulders and marched down the hallway to the spacious room that had seemed so lovely only a few hours ago; now it had the feeling of a prison cell. She slammed her suitcase onto the antique chest at the foot of the bed and began tossing her clothes into it randomly.

"Mr. Warren expects you to wait for him," Millie had said, and now Shelley mimicked her words, shoving a shoe or a purse or a piece of jewelry into the case to accent each syllable. "Well, I'm not waiting, Mr. Warren!" she spat, closing the lock with forceful gestures. "It's been fun, I suppose."

After casting one last glance at the luxurious room, she heaved the suitcase off its perch and stalked out into the hall, through the entryway and out the heavy door. She didn't even bother to check the lock as she strode purposefully toward the bank of elevators.

Tapping her foot restlessly, she punched the down button and waited for the car that would take her out of this suddenly stifling building and into the fresh air of freedom. When the doors whooshed open, Shelley looked neither right nor left, but walked into the elevator, hardly aware of the man who stepped out and then quickly jumped back inside again.

"Going somewhere, Shelley?" David asked pleasantly.

Unprepared for this development, she glared up speechlessly into his handsome face. Immediately, she was aware of his powerful presence. He seemed to fill the small space with vitality and total masculinity. Dressed in a form-fitting three-piece suit of charcoal pinstripe, he seemed not only in control of himself but capable of dominating her as well. This, she could not permit. Averting her face from his intent scrutiny, she forced herself to remember his deceptive nature as revealed by Walter Elston's recent words. A lump formed in her throat, making speech nearly impossible, but there were things that had to be said and said now.

"Our business has been concluded," she said

with what she hoped was icy reserve. "Therefore, I'm going to take care of some other business while I'm in New York and return to my
cottage. Oh, and in case you're thinking of con-
tacting me there, I'll be moving out soon. The
script will be finished in a week or two, and
there's no necessity for me to stay on at the
beach."

He studied her in speculative silence for long
seconds while the elevator descended soundlessly. At long last, he said, "I thought you'd leased
the cottage for six months. There's no need to
vacate until the lease has run out."

"You'll receive your rent!" she snapped impatiently.

"Where will you go?"

"That's none of your concern!"

"What's wrong, Shelley? Last night—"

"Last night was last night," she ground out
angrily. "Let's say it was a favor for a favor."

"A favor?" he parroted.

"Exactly. You got what you wanted. You knew
you had the part of D'Arcy, so why you arranged
the party can be your secret. I suppose it was a
means of celebrating your success, flaunting it
before your friends! As for what happened between us, it was a simple case of chemistry and
timing." Tears burned her eyelids and choked
her throat, but she went on doggedly, knowing a
sense of satisfaction when she glanced sideways
at him and spied the tensing of his square jaw,
the hurt reflected in his eyes. "You introduced
me to the right people for the movie, and I'm
grateful to you for that. You'll be pleased to know
that I've come to some decisions. I'll give the

names to my agent, who will in turn contact the proper parties." It wasn't true, but she vowed to give the matter considerable thought so that by the time she met with Walter, she would be able to supply him with the names. Even now, clouded with anger and bitterness, her thoughts were churning as she remembered the people who had been guests at the party.

"I wanted to give the party for you, to help you," he insisted. There was a tone of honest confusion in his plea, but Shelley's ears were deaf. "You seemed to need help, and it was obvious you don't know much about the film world—"

"I thought I showed my gratitude for your gracious assistance, so let's just say our relationship has come to an amicable conclusion," Shelley interrupted, unwilling to listen to any more of his soft-voiced assurances.

"You don't mean that, Shelley," he argued softly, one strong hand gripping her shoulder to send currents of fire through her entire being. "Last night should have meant more to you than—"

The elevator doors slid open, interrupting his urgent speech and revealing the hushed opulence of the vast lobby, where a half dozen people milled about.

Tossing off his restraining hand, Shelley stormed out of the elevator and crossed the carpeted lobby with what she hoped was impervious grace.

"Shelley, wait! We can't part like this!" David cried, his long legs bringing him quickly to her side. "We have to clear the air of whatever is troubling you. Please, can't we go somewhere quiet, have lunch and discuss whatever it is that's put you in this sullen mood?"

Shelley's quick steps halted. Swiveling about, she faced him. "David, don't try to charm me. I admit you deceived me up until now, but no more! You're one hell of an actor and, like all actors, you've probably talked your way out of lots of situations, but this gal isn't listening. Got it?" She paused to study his anxious face and for a fleeting moment wondered if she might have judged too hastily. He appeared so genuinely distressed, so sincere. Perhaps he didn't realize what he had done. But no, she told herself, he was first, last and always an actor and knew exactly how to convince her of his sincerity. He had used her, offered friendship and even passion, in his ruthless quest for a prized film role. And, having won that prize, he would undoubtedly be more than glad to continue their relationship to assure his success and influence over her in the future.

"I was right when I inadvertently called you Chris," she said in a low, recriminatory voice. "How I wish I had listened to my conscience and avoided you at all cost! Now . . ."

"Now?" he prompted when she broke off to bite her lower lip.

"Now, I'm a bit smarter than I was a few weeks ago!" she cried, despising the tremor that had found its way into her voice. "So this is it, chum. I'm going to walk out that door and hope I never see you or your kind again! Oh, thank you for giving the party and introducing me to so many influential people. I suppose I must say the words since you seem to have misinterpreted what happened between us last night."

She swung about, tears misting her eyes as she headed for the revolving door. Involuntarily, she cast a last glance over her shoulder and was surprised to see him standing where she had left him. His attitude was one of dejection, almost of defeat. His expression was bereft, his shoulders sagged, but he said nothing in his own defense, made no attempt to prevent her from leaving.

Impulsively, she halted with one hand resting on the door. "You may put your mind to rest about one thing, David. I've decided you were right about your precious young Jenny Sinclair. She's perfect for the role of Maryanne. She has just the right touch of sweetness enhanced by her devotion to the wrong man."

As she spun through the door, Shelley blinked back the salty tears threatening to spill over her brimming eyes, and she told herself that Jenny was a good choice, for like Shelley, the young actress had unrequited hopes of winning the love and respect of David Warren.

It was only later, seated on the plane lifting into the New York sunset, that Shelley realized she had used the term "love" to describe the feelings she and Jenny shared for the man she had just left.

Chapter Nine

"But, Shelley, I don't see why you'd pay rent for a cottage and then not use it." Darby was confused and troubled by Shelley's insistence that she was moving out of the cottage. "I don't understand any of this. You've changed so much since you came back from New York. I thought you and David Warren were . . . well . . . Oh, forget it! Why can't you stay on until the lease is up? You said the script is finished. Why don't you take some time to rest? You worked like an absolute fiend on that damned screenplay! Do you realize you never even took any time to visit with me? I thought we were friends, but whenever I called you were busy, and now that you're not busy, you're talking about moving again."

"Sorry, Darby," Shelley said, recognizing the hurt in her friend's eyes. "I really wanted to visit with you, talk about old times . . ."

"It's not too late!" Darby's eyes lost their bruised look and took on a brightness that reminded Shelley of those long-gone college years when she and Darby had been almost inseparable. "I'll make time for you. The big rush for buying and renting is over. This is the height of the season, and you really ought to take a good look at this area. People pay big bucks to come here, and they don't put out that kind of money just to stare at the ocean and fill up sheets of typing paper. Who knows, you might decide to stay here, invest in a property," she went on hopefully. "If nothing else, it'll recharge your batteries, so to speak, and with all the history in this region, you might even come up with an idea for your next novel."

Groaning, Shelley said, "Not you, too!"

"Don't tell me you're giving up writing like you gave up that TV show?" Darby was aghast, the words coming out in a disbelieving rush.

"No. I want to go on writing. It's the one thing that keeps me going, but lately everybody seems to be asking about my next book. Walter, for one. And my editor called the other day. And let's not forget little wide-eyed Jenny . . ."

Spying the curiosity flashing in Darby's eyes, Shelley broke off and averted her face.

"Who's Jenny? Someone I know?" Darby asked.

"I doubt it. She's just someone who read my book," was Shelley's evasive reply before she quickly asked, "What was that you were saying about seeing this area? Sounds like a good idea. Tell me more about it, like what's to see and when we could see it."

For the next three days Shelley and Darby toured the Delaware shore from Lewes to Fenwick Island. They laughed and talked incessantly. It was as if time had somehow been turned back and they were once again two bubbly college girls on holiday, eagerly devouring everything the coastline had to offer.

In the ancient town of Lewes, with its history of early Dutch settlers who came into the area on trading ships, they toured the historic seventeenth-century houses and Shelley filled a small notebook with historical data. Once she learned that Lewes's history was a mere eleven years younger than Plymouth, she decided the town might be of value later on should she decide to set a novel in that locale. Like schoolgirls, they licked ice cream cones while walking barefoot along the gentle beaches of Delaware Bay listening to the pulse of the waves. While eyeing the graceful sailboats skimming over the ocean, they kiddingly flirted with oystermen, clammers and crabbers, and encouraged a taciturn artist who was trying to capture on canvas the rare beauty of the landscape.

At Cape Henlopen State Park, they marveled at the wildness that had been preserved, as they discovered the extraordinary combination of ocean and bay beaches, pinelands, marshes and cranberry bogs. They investigated the "moving dunes," all that was left of a World War II army base that had controlled antisubmarine mines at the mouth of the Delaware River. Shelley became completely fascinated with these broad expanses of white rolling hills, which were capped with beach grass that gathered and held sand as it drifted northward, blown by the prevailing winds.

Touring the ivy-clad army-issue buildings dotting one section of the park, Darby whispered, "Doesn't this place give you ideas? Think of the stories you could weave around this old ghost town."

Shelley's response was an absent grunt; the seeds of a story were already sprouting in her imagination as she envisioned the area as it once must have been, bustling with activity and teeming with military characters.

Both women grew reflective when they toured the little red lighthouses at Lewes Bay and slowly strolled through the surrounding park, absorbed in the abundant wildlife. Deer peeped from the trees; quail, warblers, finches and cedar waxwings eyed the invaders with curiosity from the safety of aged trees as they pecked for food.

Without thinking, Shelley remarked, "It's so quietly scenic here. I really enjoy it. I'll bet David would like this place."

"So he's a nature lover like you?" Darby asked, her discerning regard resting on Shelley. "I'm really amazed at how much you two have in common. Too bad you can't get along."

"Drop it, Darby!" Shelley snapped, turning her attention to the landscape once more.

Following the highway that curved inland as they moved south from Lewes, they gazed raptly at the pastureland that quickly gave way to the commercialism of golden arches, trailer parks and amusement parks. Past Dewey Beach, they

continued south, covering miles of quiet coun-
tryside without saying a word. They stopped
overnight at Bethany Beach, and in the morning
they enjoyed swimming in the surf before again
heading south to Fenwick Island, which wasn't
really an island but featured an out-of-service
lighthouse that was quite a tourist attraction.
There, Shelley fell in love all over again with the
coastal waters, the juncos, hawks and egrets
which seemed offended that humans had dared
to venture into their habitat.

The trip provided a magical release from the
pressure she had been under as she'd struggled
to complete her script. It was a time for enjoying
life and restoring her mental energies, Shelley
realized, as she found herself sleeping dream-
lessly at night and awakening refreshed and
eager for the new day.

When Darby felt that Shelley had had enough
sightseeing, they headed back to Rehoboth.
There they trod streets lined with summer
homes nestled beneath tall sheltering pines and
oaks that managed to thrive only a block from
the salt water of the ocean. They rented bicycles
and headed for the busy boardwalk. Darby insisted they stop at many of the shops along the
way. Soon, Shelley found she had spent more on
clothes and jewelry than she had spent in the
past year. But she felt none of the guilt she once
might have. Instead she felt only exhilaration.
At an art gallery Shelley bought an oil landscape
that took her fancy. Darby thought it was an odd
choice since it was rendered in pale colors with
black and white predominating to create a bleak
effect.

"Why do you want that?" the real estate agent asked bluntly.

"It's a good picture of the beach, isn't it? I've loved being here, and this will be a reminder when I'm far from Rehoboth."

"If you like it so much, why leave?" Darby asked. "You've got a few months left on your lease, remember. When that runs out, I can show you some really great properties I'd love to sell to you."

Shelley chuckled. "I'll bet you could! And all of them costing the entire proceeds of my movie deal!"

"Stay on at the cottage, then," Darby coaxed. "Maybe you'll come up with another story, get a big advance and begin to look at local real estate prices as chicken feed."

"You make everything sound so simple and uncomplicated," Shelley said with a wistful smile. "You don't understand my problem, do you? After what I've learned about the owner of the cottage, I simply can't face him again. It's still his property, and I have no idea when he'll decide to just drop in like he did before. Call me a coward, but that's the way it is."

"He hasn't been here in the last month, has he?" Darby pointed out. "You haven't seen him since you left New York."

"No, but that doesn't mean he won't decide to come back. His dogs are still here, you know."

"What's that got to do with anything?"

"He's devoted to those beasts," Shelley remarked ruefully. "According to Velma and Harry, the caretakers, the dogs go everywhere with him. Since they're still at the beach, I can't help thinking he isn't far away."

"You got to like the dogs, didn't you?"

"I sure did," Shelley admitted, thinking how much more reliable animals were than humans; Fritz and Karl were certainly more worthy of trust than their master. "I even exercise them sometimes. Running along the beach with them is the way I work out and try to keep fit."

"Then maybe he left them here for you," Darby suggested. "You know, protection or company maybe, or both. He won't have much time for dogs for a while." At Shelley's questioning glance, Darby pursed her lips thoughtfully before saying, "I heard he's on his way to Hollywood to begin the film. He wouldn't take the dogs with him in a case like that, would he?"

"Who knows?" Shelley sighed wearily. "I didn't think the filming had begun already. I'm sure Walter would have let me know."

"Honey, you don't know a thing about the movie business, do you? How did you ever get to be a newswoman? I thought people in that line of work knew a little bit about everything."

"When I was a newswoman, I made it my business to know a lot about a lot of things, but I've been away from it a long time," Shelley protested quietly. "And keeping up with every move of superstars was never my big thing."

Darby grinned knowledgeably. "Let me fill you in on a few facts, then. Before a movie goes into production, there are publicity shots and costumes and things like that, all of it taking time before the actual shooting starts."

"How do you know so much about things like that?" Shelley asked doubtfully.

"I've been doing my homework," was Darby's smug reply. "I've always been interested in show biz, and since I've been handling the property of a famous star, I've made it my business to find out about these things. I'm surprised you aren't more interested in them. Not necessarily because of your association with—" she began, quickly amending that to, "Don't you care what happens to your brainchild, your book and the film?"

"Of course I do. I was only considering my own part in the writing of the screenplay, I suppose. I didn't realize things happen so fast. Let's talk about something else, shall we?"

Back at the cottage, she fixed a light lunch of salad greens and fruit for herself and Darby. It was difficult to keep her mind on the food as she picked at the lettuce in her bowl and studiously averted her glance from the cedar-sided main house, with its vast windows that seemed like eyes observing her with bemusement.

Seeing that Darby was busy consuming her salad, Shelley rose from the rattan chair to gaze out over the deserted beach, trying not to remember another time when she had strolled along the warm sand and met a most devastating man, one who had inflicted fresh wounds to her healing heart.

"Something's on your mind, Shelley," Darby remarked. "Want to talk about it?"

"I'm wondering where to go from here."

"You're really going to leave?"

"You bet!"

"So much for my sales pitch. I must be losing my touch if I can't even persuade you to stay through the season." Darby's tongue clicked against the roof of her mouth. "Ah, well, where do you think you'd like to go? Home to the family?"

"No, that's out. If I go back, even for a visit, they'll think I've given up and smother me with love and attention until I do give up. I need to be alone somewhere."

"What's wrong with right here?" Darby dared to ask.

"You're beginning to sound like a broken record," Shelley said with an amused grin. "Haven't you heard anything I've said?"

"Remember all those houses I told you about?" Darby said with an impish wink. "Some of them are being sublet for the season. What do you think?"

To placate her old friend, Shelley shrugged and said, "At this point I'm open to any reasonable suggestions. How about this afternoon? Just promise me we won't look at anything that's owned by anybody from Hollywood or Broadway."

Grinning broadly, Darby said, "Well, I was thinking of this little place along the coast that's owned by a guy with a traveling circus. He's a midget and bald. You wouldn't have a thing to worry about with him."

Laughing at her self-imposed restrictions, Shelley allowed herself to be led through a half dozen properties, each beautiful in its own way but none having quite the same sense of rightness she had experienced the first time she had

viewed David's oceanfront estate. Or had the
rightness come after she had met David? she
wondered as she gazed abstractedly at the glowing sunset from the patio of a stone structure
surrounded by tall hedges. Not one house had
an area for dogs, she observed, her thoughts
moving unwittingly to her attachment to Fritz
and Karl. A sigh escaped her lips as she again
shook her head at Darby.

"It's late and I'll bet you're hungry," Darby
said with a little too much brightness. "Let's go
all out, dress up like we used to do and go
someplace outrageously expensive where they
serve cuisine instead of food," she suggested.

"I'd like that," Shelley agreed.

On the way back to Shelley's cottage they
decided on a place specializing in Italian delica-
cies. Darby left, promising to meet Shelley at
seven sharp. Watching her drive off, Shelley
knew that their conversation would once again
center on Darby's insistence that the peace and
tranquillity available only at Rehoboth Beach
was exactly what Shelley needed, and that since
she had found nothing else, the cottage was
where she should stay.

Restless, Shelley walked through her small
temporary home, then moved onto the beach to
relive the pleasant times she had shared with
David. She wished with all her heart that those
times could have gone on uninterrupted. She
was gazing out to sea when she heard the dogs
barking excitedly. For a moment, she was certain the agitated sounds meant that David had
returned. But when silence again descended,

she concluded that some wild animal had intruded upon their territory and rouse their interest. She considered going to them, but she rejected the idea after taking a glance at her wristwatch, which told her it was time to shower and dress for the evening.

While dressing for dinner, her thoughts persisted in returning to David. It was almost as though he were nearby, so close that she could actually sense his vibrant presence, but she shuddered and chided herself for being fanciful. Still, she could not put him from her mind as she found herself pondering the significance, if any, of his absence during the past weeks. Perhaps, as Darby had said, he had gone to California to begin the preproduction business of filming *Paradise Unending*. At any event, he was not living in the imposing house, and for that she was immensely grateful.

With a light heart and a full stomach, Shelley returned to the dark cottage. Her evening with Darby had been diverting and pleasant, despite Darby's continual reminders that her lease would not run out for several months.

Paying the taxi driver, she cast an appreciative eye to the moonlit landscape and sighed, knowing that she would like nothing more than to remain there for those additional months. She could certainly use the rest, she reminded herself as she made her way up the narrow drive. Perhaps, she reasoned, Darby was right. Since David was occupied elsewhere, she had no excuse for not staying.

Slipping the key into the lock, she began to carefully consider the alternatives open to her. She could rent a luxurious apartment somewhere, buy one of those secluded homes Darby had shown her with the proceeds from the film sale, or stay here at the cottage and think about all those things later.

Not bothering to light the lamps, she moved with the slow steps of a sleepwalker through the rooms that had become dear and familiar to her. Touching the furniture lovingly, she inhaled the salty freshness that came through the open windows, heard the lulling rumble of the waves crashing against the shoreline.

Unhurriedly, she doffed her crepe dinner dress, carefully hung it on its padded hanger and arranged its voluminous folds. Next came the satin slip, the lace bra and, last of all, the sleek pantyhose. She collected a fresh silk robe and made her way to the shower, where she enjoyed a leisurely wash, following it with a brisk toweling that seemed to wake her nerve ends and leave them tinglingly alive.

Too restless to sleep, she roamed through the dark house once more until she found herself on the screened patio, admiring the serenity of the ocean with its silvery reflection of the moon's bright rays. Running her hands through her loose-flowing hair, damp from her shower, she sank into one of the rattan chairs. Leaning her head back against its roughness, she closed her eyes and allowed the peaceful night to wrap itself around her.

She had begun to doze off when she heard the

first faint strains of instrumental music. Eyes still closed, she let it filter into her consciousness, where it soothed her mind and tranquilized her tense body. Then the music soared, grew louder, more insistent, demanding her complete attention.

"Did I leave the radio on?" she quizzed herself aloud. "No, I'm sure I didn't. Now, where have I heard that before?" she mused, stirring restlessly in the chair. It was a simple melody that allowed each instrument to be heard, pure and undefiled, as it poured over her like honeyed balm.

Like invisible hands, the rhapsodic strains touched and caressed, conjured visions of a spartan room where a man could be found sitting in relaxed meditation, his elegant head resting against the tufted back of a fireside chair.

In a state of hypnotic drowsiness, Shelley's eyes opened. As if they had a will of their own, they slanted in the direction of the large house silhouetted against the velvet night sky, its lights blazing gloriously. With dreamy pleasure, she recalled the splendor of David's powerful frame, the teaklike hue of his tanned skin, the brightness of his almond-shaped eyes, the sensuous lips that curved sweetly when he smiled.

Rising from the chair, she gazed hungrily at the big house. At the very moment she realized the significance of the music, Shelley heard a whispering sound behind her. Only slightly alarmed, she swung about to peer into the darkness where a shadowy form slowly moved toward her, its outline unclear but decidedly familiar.

"So you've come back," she said in a hoarse but unemotional voice. "What do you want from me now, David?"

Chapter Ten

$\mathcal{D}$avid's soft chuckle rippled through the darkness as he approached Shelley, who stood in icy rigidity, willing herself to be unmoved by the hunger consuming her at the sight of him.

"What makes you think I want something from you?" he asked quietly. "Why can't I be here just because this is my home? I might even be here to see you and return something that belongs to you."

Shelley forced a hollow laugh and tossed her head back. "Whatever you took from me can't be returned," she said with more sharpness than she intended.

"How about this?" he asked. He was holding a garment bag that, in the silvery moonlight, appeared softly pale and ghostly, as if it had a life-force of its own. "This isn't my size and doesn't do a thing for my male image." Again, that haunting thread of laughter filtered to Shelley's ears.

Curious, she accepted the plastic bag from his outstretched hand. Turning aside, she lifted one corner to examine its contents in the moonlight that bathed the porch.

"You could turn on a light, Shelley," he suggested. "Or did you forget to pay the electric bill?"

Ignoring the remark, she moved her hands lightly in exploration of the silky garment she held. A glimmer of red brought immediate recognition, and she murmured, "This is the dress I wore to the party. I'd forgotten about it."

"Yes, that's the one." His voice was low but restrained. "As I remember, you looked beautiful in it, but not nearly as beautiful as you were a few minutes ago. Your body needs no evening gowns to bring out its loveliness."

Her head snapped upward and she was grateful for the darkness masking the flood of color that crept into her cheeks at his insinuation. "You were here when I got home tonight?" she asked with icy calm as she remembered preparing for her shower. "But, how could you have been here? Your music just started . . ."

"Timers have their uses, Shelley," he said softly. "I got home late this afternoon. You were on the beach, but by the time I got finished with phone calls and other trivial details, you had left, so I decided to wait."

"How did you get in?"

"This cottage and this property belong to me, remember? I have keys to everything."

"How could I have forgotten?" she mumbled

bitterly. Turning aside, she carefully draped the dress over the back of a chair. "Now that you've seen me and returned my party gown, you can leave."

"Not so fast," he argued gently. "Do you mind if I turn on some lights?"

"You will anyway, won't you?"

For an answer, he swung away, his athletic strides taking him into the darkness of the small house. Almost immediately, the saffron rays of a table lamp brought his virility into full view. In that instant, Shelley realized she had been holding her breath, hungrily awaiting this first glimpse of him.

Oh, but he was magnificent, she told herself silently, drinking in the sight of him. Dressed in casual trousers of beige topped by a V-necked sweater of the same neutral hue, he was a tone poem of assured masculinity. His smile was devastating, revealing even white teeth and deeply creasing dimples that tugged at her drumming heart. When he spread his arms, inviting her to step into their warmth, she staggered and almost accepted the invitation. But reason prevailed. Uttering an impatient sound, she sailed past him into the room.

"I'd offer you a seat and something to drink, but I'd rather you didn't stay that long. I'm tired and anxious to go to bed."

Ignoring her wishes, he sank into a chair facing her. "I'm anxious to go to bed too" he said, the arrogant comment softened by one of his heart-stopping smiles. "But I thought we'd talk first."

"David, I'm warning you—"

"You've warned me before," he said with a shrug before folding his arms across his wide chest. "If you recall, I wasn't frightened then, and I'm not frightened now. Haven't you learned that I do as I please?"

"I've learned that . . . among other things," was her cryptic response as she settled into the nearest chair, gathering the folds of her light-weight robe about her legs. "Let's make this short, shall we, David? What's on your mind?" To her dismay, her voice was a tremulous croak.

"I thought I'd already made that clear," he said with a lift of his arched brows. "Can we forget about the way we parted in New York and kiss and make up?"

"You've got to be kidding!"

"No, I'm not joking. I've deliberately left you alone, hoping you'd cool down and think things through logically."

Shelley fixed her gaze on him, willing herself to remain aloof from his charm. "You actually thought I was going to sit here waiting for you to come back?"

"You're here, aren't you?"

"The script took longer to finish than I had anticipated," she said, wondering why she bothered to explain herself to him. "But I handed it over to Walter when it was finally finished. Now I'm getting ready to vacate the premises."

His amused glance swept the room, took in the desk with its stack of file folders, scribbled notes and typewritten pages strewn over the surface. His eyes skimmed questioningly over Shelley's personal effects scattered about the room. "I can see that you've already begun to pack," he remarked dryly.

"Don't worry," she muttered, refusing to be intimidated by his amusement. "It won't take me long once I get at it. I can be out of here just like that!" She snapped her fingers loudly and watched the darkening of his aquamarine eyes.

"What happened in New York?" he asked, his abrupt and unexpected question catching her off guard. "What made you so mad? I'm sorry, but I still don't understand."

"You wouldn't!"

"Why don't you explain to me so that I'll understand now."

Shelley studied him through narrowed eyes, wondering if he was being completely honest with her. Was this another of his ploys to deceive through sincerity?

Realizing that there was only one way to find out, she said, "You're a very convincing actor, aren't you?"

His eyes darkened; his brows rose in question.

"You were putting on an act in New York, weren't you? The perfect host, the dear friend helping the poor befuddled author who was out of her element. Your performance was superb."

He regarded her in silence, his expression blank.

"You convinced me for quite a while. Then I learned you'd known all along that the part of D'Arcy was yours." She waited in vain for some change in David's expression. When there was none, she went on grimly, "My agent told me you knew you'd been chosen. He even told me some of your words regarding the deal. Some-thing about how pleased you were, how hard it had been winning me over since I'm a tough nut to crack!"

"I said that?" He seemed genuinely surprised. "I don't remember saying it." But he didn't deny it, she noticed. "I'm not going to lie and say I wasn't pleased when I found out you'd chosen me. After all, I'd gotten to know you, and I knew what a tough time you'd had with the casting. I figured it hadn't been an easy choice for you. Let's face it," he added with a devilishly disarm-ing grin, "with your hang-ups about those of us in the theater, you are a rather tough little nut."

"Then, if you knew you'd been chosen for D'Arcy, why all the attention?" she asked, refus-ing to submit to the sensations of pleasure that flamed through her system as she listened to his explanation. "Why the party and . . . all the rest?" she finished lamely.

"Attention?" he repeated with a shake of his head. "Are you referring to our closeness? The fact that we actually liked each other and slept together, made love?"

Grimly, Shelley nodded.

"I thought you understood my interest in you," he said, his voice a throbbing rumble that disturbed Shelley's composure and stirred unwanted memories. "I admired Shelley Tre-mayne, the author, from the time I first read *Paradise Unending*. And the young woman I met on my beach roused my desire. It seemed to me the feeling was mutual. If I was wrong, then maybe *you* should consider moving into the acting profession," he stated dryly. "As for knowing about the part and my alleged comments, let me assure you that, at the time of the party and its pleasant aftermath, I didn't know I'd gotten the part."

"Don't lie to me, David! I've been lied to by experts! Admit that the party was to celebrate your success and show your friends how completely you'd cracked this hard nut!"

"I'm not lying. Believe me, Shelley, I didn't know I'd been chosen for the part until the morning after the party. Didn't you ever wonder where I'd gone so early that morning? What had been so important that it could take me from your side?" He paused, but when she made no offer to respond, he continued to speak. "I went to confer with my manager, and it was then I received the good news. I was pleased, excited. I was so anxious to get back to the apartment and tell you how happy you'd made me—in more ways than one," he added with a twisted smile that pleaded for her understanding. "When I met you in the elevator, you dashed all my dreams, froze me out, left me confused and dazed, unable to comprehend what had gone so wrong so quickly."

"You confuse me, David. I want to believe you, but—" Shelley broke off, sinking her teeth into her lower lip and attracting his smoldering eyes to their moist softness.

"But you can't forget I'm an actor, and you're remembering another actor, aren't you? One who lied to you time and time again. How can I convince you I'm not like him?" His voice was deeply persuasive, begging for Shelley's understanding. "I'm an actor, Shelley, and proud of it and my accomplishments. But acting is the way I earn my living, not a word to describe the way I am. When the cameras stop rolling or the curtain comes down, I'm just like anybody else. Accept that I understand how you've been wounded in the past, and let's get on with living in the present."

Shelley yearned to take him at his word. She listened to his melodic voice, observed his tortured features as he implored her to believe he hadn't wronged her. Involuntarily, she rose and moved toward him until she stood over his chair, her eyes locked with his.

"But you did say I'm a tough nut to crack?" she murmured.

"Possibly," he admitted with a heavy sigh of resignation. "It's true, isn't it? Am I going to be banished from your life for a stupid remark made in the office of my business manager, a remark I can't recall?"

"I haven't decided," she replied honestly. He was so terribly attractive, so seemingly sincere in his need to be forgiven. And she remembered his look when she'd walked out on him, the dejection of his posture, the pleading message in his eyes.

"Let me help you make up your mind," he whispered hoarsely, his hands circling her small waist and tugging her downward until she was stretched across his muscular thighs, their faces close, so close that their warm breaths seemed to mingle.

"Please don't do this," Shelley pleaded.

"Why? Don't you enjoy being close to me like this?" he countered in a husky murmur. "I can't believe you don't want me to hold you, kiss you, soothe your fears. Every sweet line of your body tells me you're as eager for this as I," he went on, his hands moving with light strokes down her back, caressing the curves of her rounded hips.

"You confuse me, David."

"So you said before. Believe me, I'm confused by you, sweet Shelley."

"I doubt that anything confuses you," she said in an effort at remaining cool and composed, indifferent to his increasingly demanding and arousing touch. "You're so assured, so cool and laid-back . . ."

Grinning into her serious eyes, he taunted, "You've been reading my publicity again, haven't you? Because I don't open up to the press, reveal my innermost secrets and tell all to the yellow rags, they call me Mr. Cool."

"It suits you," she remarked, arching backward when his lips moved intimately toward hers.

"Does it?" he countered, taking her hand in his and guiding it to his chest, where her fingers felt the rapid drum of his heart beneath their timid touch. "How do you explain that?"

Searching his almond-shaped eyes, Shelley murmured, "You might just be afraid I won't believe your lies this time as easily as I did before."

"My heartbeat doesn't lie, sweet girl. Lips can lie, but mine have other things to do right now. . . ." He was whispering huskily into her parted mouth, and now his tongue darted out to circle her trembling lips, tease their softness and bring a gasp of unfeigned delight from her suddenly dry throat.

Too late, Shelley attempted to avert her mouth from his persuasive assault and felt his feverish touch against her jawbone, knew the excruciating thrill of his tongue skimming to the sensitive lobe of her ear, where it searched out the crevices to taste their particular sweetness.

, Knowing that she would be unable to hold herself aloof much longer, she pressed her palms against the unyielding hardness of his chest, relying on his sturdiness so that she could thrust herself upward and out of his embrace. Moving across the room with quick, jerky strides, she strove to collect her scrambled wits, struggled with her ragged breathing and fought for poise.

When she dared to face David, she could see that his breathing and poise were as shattered as her own, and she knew a brief moment of satisfaction. This, she was certain, was not an act; he had been not only affected by their closeness but disturbed by her abrupt rejection of his caresses. Perhaps she had been wrong in judging him so hastily, she mused. Now that she thought about it logically, it seemed he probably had been honest and sincere. It was her own distrustful heart and mind that, at the first vague hint from Walter, had leapt to conclusions, wanting to believe David possessed a devious nature.

"Tell me about California," she said, feigning nonchalance as if the last emotionally charged moments had never happened. "How are things going?"

Clearing his throat, David scowled into her flushed face. His powerful hands swept through the lush thickness of her sable hair. "If you mean the filming, we're into preproduction shots, finalizing costumes and makeup. Publicity shots have been taken, and we've done a few interviews. Laura London has been hamming it up for the gossip columnists and photographers. By the way, I think you'll be delighted with her characterization of sluttish Angelique. She's the living breathing image of your imaginary character." He paused, his eyes narrowing, and asked, "She is imaginary, isn't she? I mean, I don't have to keep glancing over my shoulder for fear of encountering the genuine Angelique, do I?"

"Are you also afraid you'll meet the real D'Arcy?" Shelley countered softly. When David's jaw tensed, she realized he still had questions and doubts about Chris. Did he expect to come face-to-face one day with the man who had inspired the fictional character? And why, she wondered, did the fantasy of seeing the two of them together, of making comparisons, cause her heart to pound? "Angelique is totally from my imagination. I needed a way to explain D'Arcy's character. As real as he is . . . was . . . to me when I wrote my novel, I felt the readers would find him unbelievable if I didn't show how he became the person he is."

"Well, I can't help but wonder," he mumbled, rising to pace the floor restlessly. "The studio writers and bosses are putting some odd touches on some of your characters, you know. Angelique's is only one."

"Do you think my screenplay has been altered?"

"I'm not saying that, because I don't know if it's true. You haven't kept a close watch on your script since turning it in, have you?" David asked cryptically.

"Well, no, I haven't," Shelley admitted. "I expected Walter to look out for my interests and handle everything."

"Perhaps you ought to check with him again," David suggested. "Maybe he doesn't know everything that's been happening out in Los Angeles."

Shelley studied David closely. A growing concern swept over her, and she channeled her attention on the man who paced before her like a caged cat. "But, I don't understand. Why should I be worried about the script?" she asked quietly. "It's still my script, isn't it?"

"I honestly don't know," David repeated, halting his prowling steps to face her across the expanse of the room. "I never read your screen version until I got out to L.A., but I had read the book. Many times, in fact," he pointed out with a shy smile. "Somehow, I felt certain that your script would follow the novel faithfully, but—"

"But the script you're using in Hollywood doesn't follow the book," she finished for him. "That's what you're saying, isn't it?"

A noncommittal shrug was his only response as his eyes held her worried gaze. After a considerable time, he looked away, allowing his glance to sweep the room curiously. "You say you're preparing to move out?" he asked thoughtfully.

"Yes. It won't take long, believe me," she

replied, disturbed by his obviously deliberate change of topic. She wondered if, after having brought up the script, he was now evading her pointed question. Had he said something he shouldn't have?

"Where are you going?" he asked.

"Is it important to you?"

"It could be important to you," he replied enigmatically.

"In what way?" Her tone was lifeless, almost disinterested. How quickly his desire for her had cooled, she observed mutely while admitting she probably was at fault. She had, after all, deliberately rejected his warm embrace, his teasing kisses, hadn't she?

"If you have no special commitments anywhere, you might find a trip to the West Coast interesting. Have you ever been to Hollywood?"

"Yes. A long time ago." Odd, she mused. Recollection of that one disastrous trip to visit Chris while he had been filming his sci-fi epic usually caused physical pain; now, there was just a vague emptiness in her heart. "I didn't like the climate," she added with a mirthless chuckle.

"Things might be different now," he said with genuine warmth. "I mean, it seems natural that you'd like to see the filming of your book. You might even find yourself wanting to watch this humble actor at work," he added with a shy smile. "Should that become boring, there are lots of sights to see along the coast. The early shooting is being done on the studio sound stages, but later we'll be moving to northern California to shoot the tropical scenes, where I do my dastardly deeds."

His dry humor was not wasted on Shelley, who smiled broadly and warmed to his suggestion. She told herself it might be exciting to watch him at work, to be with him again, however briefly or impersonally. There was no denying his attractiveness, his pull on her emotions.

"Where in northern California? I'm starting to get interested—in seeing my book come alive," she explained innocently, adding, "Do you think I'd get the chance to sit and talk with the director and producer? It sounds as if I might have some . . . suggestions to make after I see what they've been doing."

"I'm sure that can be arranged. As for the location shots, they're scheduled for next month up around Carmel, in some of the lush areas along the coast."

"I've heard it's beautiful."

"You've never been there, though?"

"No."

"I live not far from Carmel," he stated, the corners of his lips tilting upward in a beguiling smile. "It's a big house nestled in the trees. A writer would probably find it an ideal spot to work."

"Are you inviting me to visit you at your California home?" How many homes did this man have? she wondered, warming beneath his steady gaze and overt teasing. She was curious about his West Coast dwelling. Would it be as impressive as this lovely house on the Delaware coast?

"I'm *offering* you my home," he corrected softly. "I'll be working long hours and won't be there. The studio gives me a trailer when we're on location. My home is on the edge of Point Lobos State Park, some distance from where we'll be shooting, so I'll be stuck, I'm afraid."

"I see."

The knowledge that he was offering her his home but not his disturbing presence was disappointing to Shelley, who had begun to think it might be possible to be friends with him after all. Friends, but nothing more, she cautioned her beating heart. Still, he would have to come home once in a while, wouldn't he? she argued with herself. And during those visits, wasn't it possible that they might return to their former easiness with each other, assuming she could forget her suspicions and come to trust him completely.

"Are all of your homes substitute hotels for your friends? And how many do you have?" she asked boldly. Spying his startled expression, she laughed and said, "Homes, that is."

"This is my home base, believe it or not. The New York apartment is a convenience. I prefer the Broadway stage to the glitter of the film world, but work is work. The house at Point Lobos is relatively new," he explained glibly. "You see, to keep working, I made a number of rather bad movies where I played second banana to giant spiders and the like. The pay was good and I still get royalties when they show up on late-night TV. For a while, it looked as though I'd be doing more of them, so I built a retreat where I could live in quiet obscurity." He paused, watching her reaction, as he decided just how much he should reveal. "I really thought I'd go on to fame and outrageous for-

tune as the king of the monster movies, but then
the artist in me got in the way. I decided I was
rich enough to be selective in my work, so I
made up my mind to contract only for films of
artistic value. That explains all the classics and
historical epics. They may not make me as rich
as the horror flicks, but they've given me a
reputation I can be proud of."

Shelley was moved by the wistful tone that
had crept into his voice. She could tell that his
decisions had been a trial for him, and she
searched for a way to reassure him. "With a
talent like yours, what did you really have to
prove? You always had your stage work, didn't
you? Directors surely saw you for what you were,
didn't they? Why the need to impress with
wealth and riches?"

Lowering his glance, David offered no reply.
Instead, he said, "Will you come to California?
Take me up on my offer of the Point Lobos
house? I'd like to know it won't always be empty
while I'm on the Coast. Your presence would
brighten even that sunny site." His voice cajoled, caressed and warmed Shelley's ears,
swept away her doubts and lingering fears.

"I'll think about it," she said, remembering
the lovely summer outfits she had bought in
Rehoboth, the perfect wardrobe for California's
sunny climate. She was also envisioning the
confrontation that would surely take place
should she learn that the studio had tampered
with her script.

"I wish you would," he murmured huskily,
advancing until he stood before her, his hands
resting lightly on her upper arms. "We can be

friends, if that's all you want, Shelley. Believe me."

His head dipped slowly, his glittering eyes never once releasing their hold on hers. When his lips touched her parted mouth, it was with such sweetness that she felt a twinge in her heart. But when her fingers sought to link behind his dark head, he moved slightly. His hands cupped her chin, and he whispered, "I'll leave you to do your thinking. Good night, my sweet Shelley."

With a gentle motion, he freed himself from her arms and disappeared into the darkness of the night.

Chapter Eleven

For Shelley, the trip to Hollywood was like reliving a nightmare. Although it had been years since she had been to the fabled Tinseltown, little had changed, she quickly discovered. Beneath the golden California sun, there was still the same fury of sound and activity. There was still too much of everything, she noticed immediately. Too much glamour, too many California girls with their toothy smiles and shapely tanned bodies, too many golden boys flexing their muscles as they made their way to the surf with gleaming surfboards tucked under their bare arms, too much canned music, too much false gaiety and charm. The skimpily clad people strolling aimlessly along the palm-lined walks and sunning themselves to a nut brown with lazy concentration pursued a lifestyle she could not understand.

Despite the outward show of laid-back relaxation and inviting opulence, Shelley knew the same horrors she had experienced so long ago still lay beneath the dazzling glitter and golden gloss. Numbed to the tropical paradise around her, she shopped alongside famous personalities selecting fresh fruits and vegetables in the outdoor markets, made a concerted attempt at eating raw fish, even spent her quota of hours in the sun watching her freckles increase. Most of the time, she managed to ignore the peculiar excitement that hung in the air like a living presence. Everywhere she went, she searched the faces of strangers, those she passed on the crowded streets, in the sumptuous hotel where she was staying, at the studio where *Paradise Unending* was being filmed; that she expected to encounter Christopher Devon and his horde of hangers-on, she did not deny. And when she didn't, the sense of relief was remarkable in its encompassing sweetness.

Were it not for David's comforting presence, his aura of protective, almost boyish, pleasure in showing her the sights, in guiding her through the vast maze of the studio, in attempting to make her feel less of an outsider in the land of make-believe, Shelley was certain she would have turned tail and run. Frequently, in the solitude of her hotel room, she asked herself why she had agreed to this madness. What demon had possessed her, influenced her to go against her better judgment and embark on this nightmare.

The answer, always the same, rang clear in her mind: she had wanted to come, wanted to be near David Warren, wanted to view the film-making process at close range, wanted to see her screenplay brought to life before her eyes. It never occurred to her to question the order of her desires, to wonder why the screenplay came last, for during those last days at Rehoboth Beach, ecstatically memorable days spent in David's exhilarating company, she had come to accept their friendship and easiness with each other. With each passing day, she had looked to him more and more for guidance and listened in awe to his knowledgeable explanations of the technicalities of film making. Warming to his gentleness, she had forgotten her mistrust of him and all those in his profession, and shared with him her uncertainties about her new career. And all the while, she pondered the hints he threw out that the screen version was to be a deliberate deviation from what she had submitted.

When David left Rehoboth Beach for California, his parting words had been ones of friendship and comaraderie. His greatest hope was that Shelley would decide to visit the film capital, spend a few weeks there and move on with the company when it went north for location shots. When he reiterated the offer of his Point Lobos home as a refuge, Shelley had shyly told him to expect her soon.

Alone at the beach house, Shelley had finally acknowledged that, despite her good intentions and better judgment, she had succumbed to an almost obsessive infatuation for David. Pondering the outcome of such a foolish obsession, she convinced herself that she was simply a normal female attracted to the glamour and success surrounding a rising star. As for the future, she gave it little consideration. She and David truly enjoyed each other, understood and admired their separate talents, and knew how to coddle one another's idiosyncracies. Shelley reminded herself that theirs was a relationship that might last through the timetable of the filming, but would undoubtedly end when the movie was wrapped up and turned over to the distributors. That, Shelley told herself, would be enough.

Shelley's life in California was made pleasant only by her daily visits to the studio, where she ate hurried lunches with a David she barely recognized in his newly acquired beard and theatrical makeup. Observing the camera crew, the script girls, the extras, the name stars and bit players was an experience she enjoyed more than she would have thought possible. Everything seemed to be exciting, she noticed, from the first day of standing silently on the sidelines of the amazingly realistic sets. Since there was no continuity to the shooting, she could not tell immediately if her script was being used. Scenes were enacted and filmed at random according to the needs of the director, who had mapped out the schedule and kept his crew hopping through the long grueling days of shooting and re-shooting the same scene until he was satisfied.

"Do you understand everything you're seeing?" David asked of Shelley as he picked at a fruit salad in the commissary. His jewel-like eyes, emphasized by expertly applied makeup, searched hers. "I realize you know we're doing indoor scenes, but have you been able to tell where we are in the script?"

"Not really," Shelley admitted, pushing her empty yogurt container to one side. "I'd like to see the final shooting script, but I guess I've been asking the wrong people for one. All I've seen are loose pages of dialogue left lying around the set. They don't help at all."

David flashed his boyish grin. "If you promise not to tell anybody, I'll let you borrow mine." Lowering his voice, he leaned toward her. "I have an uncut, unscrambled copy."

"Doesn't everybody in the cast have the full script?" Shelley asked, amazed at the way he managed to make her nerve ends tingle with his teasing smile, the low confidentiality of his voice. With his sunbrowned hand resting only inches from hers, it required supreme control to restrain herself from stroking those long shapely fingers.

"Some do," David replied. "Most of the bit players get only their scenes, though, which is probably what you've managed to pick up around the set. Would you like to see my copy?"

"After all the hints you've tossed my way, letting me think my work has been tampered with, I'm dying of curiosity and you know it!" she replied.

"Busy tonight?"

Was he going to make arrangements to be with her later? Dare she allow him to know how much she would like that? Dropping her thick lashes over her eyes to shade the glow she knew was shining there, she managed to say with teasing lightness, "I was going to swim with Clint tonight, but that was before Dustin called. Eastwood and Hoffman have been battering down my door since I registered at the hotel, you know. It's a terrible burden, being so in demand! And then I was invited to the party at Liz's place in Beverly Hills . . ."

"Would it be okay if I brought the script to the hotel? I wouldn't want to interrupt anything or keep you from getting to Liz's on time, of course," he said with a crestfallen, apologetic air as he fell into her teasing mood.

"Oh, please don't worry about that, my dear," Shelley said, continuing the banter. "Come whenever you have the time. I realize how precious your free time is to you." She spied the glint of laughter in his bright eyes and felt her heart turn over in her breast.

With all the teasing in the air, Shelley was unprepared when David quickly grasped her slender wrist and said with heartrending solemnity, "I'll come whenever you tell me to." He fell silent, waiting for her answer, but Shelley was tongue-tied, unsure of how to respond. The moments dragged on, and then David dropped her hand and, lowering his voice to a sober monotone, said, "Would it suit you if I come when I've finished with the day's shooting?"

"Providing you dispense with that dreadful greasepaint," she replied in a faltering falsetto that she hoped disguised the breathless anticipation she was experiencing. Lowering her voice to its normal range, she asked, "Seriously,

David, if you're too tired, don't bother. I can pick up the script at your dressing room before I leave the studio."

"Please, no. Not when I'm so anxious to be alone with you. I've missed our evening chats, haven't you?" Was it her imagination or had his resonant voice taken on a note of wistfulness?

She didn't know if he was still acting or had decided to be serious. Should she admit to him how much she had missed those quiet talks they had enjoyed at the beach, the shared intimacy that had given purpose to the languid summer days and had been noticeably absent from their relationship since her arrival on the Coast?

"Come whenever you can," she said quietly, dropping her eyes from his penetrating glance but allowing her fingers to intertwine with his as she savored the warmth flowing from him into her. "I'm not going anywhere, and I don't usually go to bed early."

He laughed. "I'm glad. I was so afraid that you were planning on a night of revelry with Clint *and* Dustin, in which case I'd leave the script at the desk for delivery at an appropriate time." Sobering, he said, "I'll try to get away from the studio early, get cleaned up, change and be at your hotel in time for a late supper. Are you agreeable to that?"

"It sounds lovely." Shelley sighed, pleased to know that they would be together soon, away from the eyes of the studio bosses, free of the restraints that pervaded its bustling halls.

The late supper turned out to be an intimate midnight feast of asparagus quiche and a tossed salad of lettuce, spinach and endive mounted with fresh fruit, washed down with sparkling Burgundy and topped off with a mellow Camembert. They ate in the privacy of Shelley's spacious hotel room, the candles on the portable dining table providing soft illumination while millions of twinkling lights in the Hollywood Hills gleamed through the velvet darkness to provide a romantic backdrop. Their low-voiced conversation avoided film making entirely. They were two adults, a man and a woman enjoying a sumptuous meal together, casting curious glances at each other and laughing easily.

The time flew by until, replete with good food and warmed by the wine, the hushed atmosphere and David's admiring glances, Shelley rose from the table to gaze absently through the window onto the starlit night landscape.

"Ready to talk about the script, Shelley?" David asked. His footsteps hushed by the thick carpeting, he had come to stand behind her. His warm breath feathered her ear as he spoke; his hands rested lightly on the curve of her waist. His presence, their closeness, stirred thoughts that were a far cry from the screenplay that had brought them together. "I thought you'd pounce on it and go over it immediately, but you seem reluctant to even look at it."

"I am, David," she whispered, her eyes darting to the bound screenplay still lying on the satin bedspread where she had placed it in her eagerness to see David again, to hear his voice, observe him across the table from her while they ate. "I'm not sure I'm ready to find out it's been changed."

"Sooner or later, you're going to have to read it," he murmured huskily, his hands gripping her by the shoulders to spin her so that they faced each other. His smiling eyes brought an answering quiver to her soft lips. She yearned to prolong the air of intimacy that still permeated the room, caused her blood to race and made her heart thunder as it beat restlessly against her rib cage.

"Do I have to read it right now? While you're here?" she asked, adding silently, Do I have to share even these private moments with the studio? Can't we have a few hours of relaxed friendship as we used to have?

"We'll read it together," he suggested, gently lowering her to the roomy love seat beneath the wide window. "I'll act it out for you, if you'll feed me the lines."

"That sounds like fun," Shelley said, attempting to generate some enthusiasm. Leaning back against the sofa, she followed him with her eyes as he strode with casual grace to the bed, picked up the screenplay and returned to lower himself beside her. "I'm not much of an actress," she pointed out when he flipped the script open and commenced to read the cast of characters in his mellow baritone.

Spreading the book across their two laps, he grinned into her wide eyes and said, "I'll try to remember that, but I've always suspected that writers have secret dramatic ambitions that they vent through the printed word." He went on to describe the opening scene with a flair that won an amused chuckle from Shelley, who was completely entranced by his reading, his closeness, his compelling masculinity.

"So far, so good," she said, painfully conscious of his muscled thigh pressing against the silken softness of her crimson dress, and wondering if he shared her awareness. "Read on."

By the time they had enacted almost a third of the script, Shelley was convinced that there were numerous changes, some glaring, many subtle, all altering the inherent motivation, the crisp characterizations she had created so lovingly and well.

Their reading had been half in fun, half in earnest. At times, she had become lost in wonder, so caught up in the spell of David's flawless delivery that he had to remind her that it was her turn to read. But now she came to rigid attention, her fingers flipping through the printed pages, her eyes skimming over the dialogue that was not hers and bore little resemblance to her work. The fury and humiliation she felt brought tears to her eyes as she acknowledged the truth about the words shimmering before her.

"It isn't your screenplay, is it?" David's question was quietly voiced, without inflection or emotion. His serious eyes regarded her with compassion. "The studio put their own writers to work on it without telling you."

"Can they do that? Will it do me any good to complain?" she cried, her hands trembling as she continued to leaf through the script. "Why have they done this? Why did they want my book if this is what they had in mind? This isn't even the same story!"

"Shelley, these things happen," David soothed, his hands covering hers and stilling their agitated restlessness.

Allowing his warmth to seep into her through the touch of his hands on hers, Shelley gazed into his concerned eyes and longed to turn back the clock to those blissful shared minutes at dinner when they had been relaxed, at ease with each other, untroubled by outside forces, unconcerned about the script or the will of studio heads.

"David, what can I do?" she whispered desperately, pleading for his strength as well as his advice. "I don't want my story changed. Not like this!" Her forefinger tapped the pages. "Tell me what to do, whom to complain to! There has to be someone who can do something!" Her voice rose hysterically as a new idea occurred to her. "There is something I can do about this, isn't there? It isn't too late?"

David's strong hand cupped her trembling chin, and a long forefinger traced the outline of her cheek, brushed a stray strand of hair as he whispered, "No, it isn't too late. Why do you think I insisted you come here? Why do you suppose I brought the script to you? I wanted you to see for yourself what's happening. I thought you ought to know about it because it seemed to me that most of the changes ruined your story."

"You really care, don't you?"

"Sure, I care."

"Why do you care so much?" she asked, confused by the flood of emotions chasing through her system—anger at the studio with its stable of hack writers; fear of the moneyed men who had backed this abortion of her work; distrust of Walter Elston, who had negotiated the motion picture deal; warmth and affection for this man beside her, whose soft eyes soothed her, whose hands touched her with fire and whose voice could both calm her fears and stir her passions. "What does it matter to you whose words you speak before the camera?" she probed.

"I care, Shelley. Your book was a damned good one, and I'm sure your script was just as good, maybe better. Selfishly, I'm very selective about my work, and I went to a lot of trouble to surround myself with capable people, not only actors but technical staff, so that this would be one of my best works, if not the best. I don't want it to bomb with the critics or at the box office."

His voice, low and sincere, mesmerized Shelley, whose eyes had filled with salty tears of frustration and disappointment. She had hoped David would say he cared about *her,* about her artistic stature. Despite his honesty, she felt betrayed by his explanation. Clearing her throat, she moved her head just enough so that his light grip on her chin was released.

"These people you've surrounded yourself with," she said, swallowing back the hot tears threatening to spill over at any moment, "have any of them got any say about the script?"

"Not really, but I know someone who does. I've already laid the groundwork, but I haven't the same clout as you."

"Really?" she laughed mirthlessly. "I didn't

think I had any clout at all, whereas you, being the great superstar—"

"Shelley, I'm only an actor. We actors may try to impress the writing staff with our importance, but they know we do it simply because we want our scenes to be better. We don't carry much weight with them. But a woman like you, the author of the novel the film is based on, might stand a chance of impressing the bosses. I can arrange a meeting for you, but that's all I can do."

"That's all?" she asked with a twisted smile. "I can't get a meeting set up on my own, so I'd say that was something. Will you do it? Put in a word and get me an appointment?"

"Of course I will. When would be the best time for you?"

"As soon as possible, before the whole story is filmed and my story line is ruined. Can you arrange something for, say, tomorrow? Or within the week?"

"I can certainly try," he assured her. "What's the sense of having influence if I never use it?"

Laughing, Shelley shook her head in wonder. "I'm so glad I have you, David. I mean, how would I ever find my way around this jungle without your guidance?"

David put an arm around her shoulders to draw her close. "You do have me, Shelley; make no mistake about that. I'm not about to let you wander around alone in the jungle. There are too many wild animals lurking behind the trees in search of unwary prey like you."

Tilting her head back, she gazed up into his face. "What does that mean?" she whispered throatily. Did it mean that he cared about her? she mused pensively.

"It means, Shelley, love, that I've decided to protect you from the dangers of this counterfeit world we're both living in. I know some of them, and you're finding out about a few. If I have any say about it, I'm not going to let you be led down a path that leads to oblivion, not by the studio or the writers and certainly not by any devious actors, got it?"

Although she regretted that his assurances were motivated by nothing but friendship, his words made her heart rejoice. Placing her head against his shoulder, she inhaled the familiar male scent of him and grew dizzy with longing for more than the casual hug he offered. A sigh escaped her parted lips, and she could not control its wistful sound.

"Tired?" he asked. His deeply resonant voice throbbed with concern as his beard grazed her temple.

"Not really. Mentally exhausted, maybe. But you're probably dead tired, aren't you?" she asked, glancing up into his face to study the lines of weariness etched around his eyes, alongside his sensual lips. "I never realized what long days actors put in," she remarked thoughtfully.

"You mean Chr . . . you've never been exposed to an actor at work before?" he amended quickly, his fingers gripping her shoulder and holding her against him when she would have broken free of his light embrace.

"No, not really. The only time I was in Hollywood, I stayed at my hotel. I didn't go to any of the studios, so I didn't realize what goes into making a movie." She grew quiet, not knowing what to say, not wanting to drift into painful recollections of that other visit or the man who had inspired it. "For instance, I never knew the cast and crew put in such long hours. Why, do you realize it was almost midnight when you got here? And I imagine you'd been working since before dawn."

"If you're wondering if I'm about to fold my tent and steal away so that I can be rested for tomorrow morning, let me assure you that being with you is as restful as a full night's sleep," he said with warmth and a smile that lit up his aquamarine eyes.

Uncertain whether she should be offended or pleased by his comment, Shelley offered no remark of her own. She had been complimented on many things, her intellect, her education, her serene good looks, even her conversational abilities, but never had she been deemed as restful as a night of sound sleep!

"Just being with you like this," David was saying, his voice low and compelling with his lips a hairsbreadth from her earlobe, "is one of life's little luxuries. Even if we never said a word, I could sit here with you all night and go to work rested and ready for action."

Irritated by his quiet words, Shelley stirred in his embrace. "Maybe I should have given more consideration to Clint's invitation," she murmured, casting a curious glance at him from the corner of her eye and knowing a smug sense of satisfaction when he frowned his displeasure.

"Am I boring you?" he asked gruffly.

"No, not at all," was her nonchalant response

as she lifted her head and turned so that she could observe the night skyline. The magic she had seen in the sparkling lights dotting the velvet blackness had faded, leaving only a gaudy display stretching to infinity. "Did you ever notice that all cities look alike at night? It's as if the darkness hides their grimy imperfections," she said absently.

Shifting so that he too could gaze out over the sprawling city, David murmured his agreement. "From that remark, I doubt you'll miss all this glamour when we move north. You are going with the company, aren't you?"

"A lot depends on that meeting you're going to set up for me," she replied listlessly.

Shelley's head swiveled toward him at the same moment his attention focused on her. Like two comics in a vaudeville routine, their foreheads and then their noses bumped crudely. Discomfited and embarrassed, they grunted and then began to laugh. Dropping her head onto David's chest, Shelley allowed the amusement to wash away her unreasonable animosity and doubts until she was once again beguiled by the scent and feel of the man whose arms had quickly closed about her.

"Ah, Shelley, you are a wonder! When I need you, you're there. I hope I can always be here when you need me. Is that asking too much?"

"You need me?" she echoed disbelievingly.

"I needed you tonight, and here you are," he said, squeezing her upper arm with gentle affection.

"What do you need me for?"

"You don't know?" he whispered, gathering

her close and tipping her head back so that his penetrating gaze could hold hers.

Sighing, Shelley watched as his features came close, his unblinking eyes filling her world, warming her with their brightness.

His lips took hers in gentle possession, eliciting an eager response, then moved to rain tender kisses on the tip of her small nose, the thin bridge between her closed eyes, her eyelids, forehead, the soft tendrils of hair haloing her face. The silky softness of his beard tickled Shelley's flesh, but rather than finding the sensation annoying, she experienced a growing excitement. Her fingers toyed with it, explored it curiously as his mouth claimed hers again and his rough tongue darted between her parted lips to search the moist sweetness inside.

Hungrily, Shelley returned his provocative caresses, tasted his maleness and felt desire uncoil from the center of her being until she was afire with raw need. When his fingers stroked her into pliant submissiveness, she molded herself to him, savored the hardness of his muscular virility. Their combined passion seemed to mount until it blazed with a heat that could not be doused. Twisting in his arms, she opened herself to his searching lips and hands, offered no protest when his stroking fingers worshiped her body, leisurely explored her curves, aroused and awakened emotions that cried out for expression.

With love consuming her, pouring over her like warm honey, she soared to ever higher levels of rapture until every part of her body felt as if it were afire. Breathing in soul-drenching gasps, her hands swept upward until her fingers latched on to the lapels of his summer-weight sport jacket. With light feathery movements, she slid the jacket backward, down over his muscular arms, and knew delight when he shrugged free of the garment. Lips still joined, she let her fingers undo the small buttons of his crisp linen shirt so that they might roam unimpeded over the downy hairs of his naked chest. Exulting in the sheer maleness surrounding her, she allowed her hands to fondle his nipples in the same way his fingers were toying with the sensitive pebbles of her breasts through the fabric of her silk gown. When her fingers explored further, lower, across the hard planes of his flat stomach, then down to the tensed muscles of his thighs, she heard the muffled moan that came from deep in his throat. Leaning against him, she circled his lips with the tip of her tongue, memorized each sensual contour as she wallowed in her control over this dynamic man.

"Oh, God, Shelley, don't . . ." he muttered hoarsely, his hands moving with agility over the smoothness of her gown, stroking and caressing the curves that lay just beneath its silkiness. "Don't tease me . . ."

"Who's teasing?" she whispered against his parted lips.

Her body vibrated with the force of her need. Wanting nothing more than to surrender to the sweetness of his masterful touch, to know again the soul-shattering ecstasy of his lovemaking that still lived in her memory, she smiled dreamily when his hands lifted the hem of her dress and eased it above her hips to allow him access to the throbbing femininity he sought. When his light touch feathered over the flesh of her thighs, she shuddered in anticipation and lifted her arms so that he could at last remove the gown completely.

As he slid the dress off her shoulders, his eyes skimmed over her trembling curves and a tormented groan slipped through his lips. Gripping her by the waist, he placed her against the cushions of the love seat and leaned over her. His breathing was ragged, his expression intense. Gazing hotly into her flushed face, he mutely questioned her willingness to pursue their lovemaking to its proper conclusion. Sensing his doubt, Shelley arched upward in mute invitation, but still he hesitated.

"I need you, David . . ." she crooned. "I need to be loved again. Please—"

"Shelley, I want you, God knows I do, but I can't forget the last time, the way you turned on me." He paused, and his eyes searched her passion-glazed features, roamed hungrily over the creamy expanse of trembling flesh before him, crying out for his touch, for release, and he groaned as if in pain. "Maybe later, when you've had time to think, after you've settled the question of the script, once you're relaxed and rested, comfortable at Point Lobos, forgotten . . ."

His words, halting and reflectively quiet, took Shelley by surprise. He couldn't be rejecting her! But he was! After rousing her to throbbing awareness, taking her to the dizzy edge of insanity, he was turning away!

"Please, David, I need you," she pleaded, her

hands linking behind his head, pulling him down to her so that she could press hungry bruised lips to his hard mouth, impress upon him the extent of her desire, her need. For a moment, his lips returned her insistent pressure, but then he drew back. Shaking his head, he released her. His fingers closed over her upper arms and urged her to relinquish her hold on him.

"No, Shelley, not now, not tonight. You don't need me. No, don't say anything, don't argue. You're too vulnerable. You're remembering another time, another man who hurt you, and you want to get even. I have memories too, and I remember a night when you came to me, willingly and wantonly, but your mind was somewhere else. You were thinking of someone else."

"What are you saying?" she cried, confused.

"I'm saying that your visit here is bringing back old memories. The problems with the studio writers isn't helping matters. Making love with me won't solve the problems eating at you." Rising, he began to restore order to his disheveled clothing. "I'm beginning to think I was wrong in coming here tonight, in telling you about the rewrite job. I probably should have let you visit the set, observe the filming and find it out for yourself. Let's say good night and part as friends. We are friends, aren't we?" Leaning toward her, he extended his hand to cup her chin, force it upward.

"Friends?" she echoed inanely, flipping her face sideways to throw off his touch. "That's a strange word to describe two people who have just started to make love and ended arguing pointlessly!" she snapped irritably, pulling herself up and off the love seat. She bent to retrieve her discarded dress, then struggled to pull it over her head, unaware that she had donned it backward as she spun about to glare at the man quietly buttoning his shirt. "You are going to make that appointment for me, aren't you?" At his nod, she pressed, "Do you still want me to go to Point Lobos? Or are you afraid there will be bad memories there? If there are, my *friend*, they'll be yours and not mine!"

Disregarding her angry outburst, he said sincerely, "I'm looking forward to having you there. Did you think my mind had changed just because I refuse to accept your body when you're upset and confused?"

"I'm confused?" she flared hotly. "I'd say you're the one who's confused, David. You say you want me, you claim you are looking forward to my visit at Point Lobos, that we're friends, and yet—"

"And yet I realize how upset you are, dear Shelley, how vulnerable. Think about it. A little while ago, you were outraged at the studio for tampering with your script; then you were tired and concerned for my weariness. As if to clear your troubled spirit, you teased me into making love to you, but when I was reluctant to pursue the matter, you became angry again."

Offended by the underlying truth of his words, Shelley turned away. What hurt most was the suggestion that she was remembering Chris. Unable to face the sadness clouding his glowing eyes, reflections of her own misery, she was equally unwilling to see him shrugging into his jacket and preparing to leave her.

"You'll be on the set tomorrow?" he asked, one hand resting lightly on the doorknob.

"I suppose so. When will you know about the conference I hope to have with whoever it is you're arranging for me to meet?" She could not disguise the sullen belligerence lacing her question.

"By noon tomorrow, I hope," he replied quickly. "By the way, in case you think I'm being secretive, I'm going to arrange for you to meet with the associate producer and the head of the script department. They're the only ones who can do anything tangible. Meanwhile, get some rest." He considered her downcast features and said with extreme gentleness, "I do want you, Shelley. I just don't want you out of gratitude or some other misguided motivation. You do understand, don't you?"

Numbly, she met his steady glance and nodded. She understood, all right, she told herself silently; he wanted her, desired her, but did not love her. His desires and wants were only tools with which to control her, to be slaked when he chose. He was nothing more than a selfish, self-centered actor, and the sooner she accepted that fact, the better off she would be.

"See you tomorrow, Shelley," he whispered. He leaned toward her and brushed his lips against hers with the casualness of an old friend, but the light caress did nothing to ease the pain stabbing at her heart.

Chapter Twelve

To Shelley's chagrin, David's work schedule kept him out of her life for several days. At first, she thought he was deliberately avoiding her, but after visiting the studio a few times, she realized that he was under tremendous pressure.

She was even more distressed that the filming was continuing without interruption despite her request for a meeting with the studio heads. When she could no longer bear the uncertainty, she sent a message to David, asking him to meet her for lunch.

"Did you speak to the studio people at all?" she demanded to know as soon as they sat down at the lunch table.

Patiently, David explained that he had followed through on her request and been assured that a meeting would be scheduled. "They didn't say when," he admitted, avoiding her sharp eyes as he gave his attention to a rather dry-looking cube steak.

"But they're still shooting!" she protested, leaning across the Formica table to peer into his face. "They're still using that script that makes my story seem like a melodramatic farce!"

"I know. What do you want me to do?" he asked wearily, lifting his eyes to meet her accusing glance. "Do you think it's my fault they rewrote the script?"

"No, of course not," she mumbled. "I'm just afraid I won't get to meet with those people and have my say about it before too much of the movie is filmed."

Spearing a mound of mashed potato, David plopped it into his mouth and then turned to Shelley. "Don't let that bother you. We keep shooting because we're following a schedule. Even if you manage to convince the director and his pals to change the script, we may still be able to salvage some of what we're filming now." He paused to consider her and, as if sensing that he had spoken too curtly, patted her hand and said, "Relax, Shelley. It'll all work out. Say, why don't you do something to keep your mind busy while you're waiting?"

"Like what?" She wanted to say that, without him beside her, nothing was interesting, but she held her tongue, waiting for him to come up with some dynamic suggestion or to say he would find the time to be with her. Observing him as he considered her terse question, she saw for the first time the tense lines about his mouth, the puffiness beneath his eyes that hadn't quite been masked by stage makeup, and she felt remorse for her selfish desire to be with him.

"You're in Tinseltown, aren't you? Some of the most beautiful people in the world live and work here, and that attracts a lot of tourists. Most people who come here want to see the homes of the stars. Aren't you even a little bit interested in seeing some of those fantastic houses? They are fantastic, you know; it's no exaggeration."

"I'm not—," she began, only to be hushed by his hand gripping her chin and his forefinger stilling her lips.

"I know you're not interested in stars or their homes, but you're a writer, aren't you? Some of those mansions are pretty interesting and have a lot of history behind them."

The only home she was interested in was his, she replied mutely; the only history, the ongoing saga of her abandoned script. Aloud, she scoffed, "You don't really think I'll come up with a dynamite idea just from looking at some far-out architecture, do you?"

"You might. Why not give it a try?" His finger was still moving, lightly caressing her chin. "Shelley, I'd love to go with you, but I'm tied up right now. We've been working from four in the morning until midnight this last week and I'm bushed!"

Again she experienced guilt. He was working so hard, and all she could do was hope he would find time for her. To cover her feelings, she said, "Four in the morning! Why start so early?"

Preening his trim beard, he flashed a warm grin. "Makeup takes at least an hour, and then there's the costumes and setting the lights. Want to hear more?"

"No. I'm sorry you're so worn out," she said with genuine concern. It tugged at her heart to see him so exhausted.

"You ought to be sorry," he said lightly, again gripping her chin and giving it a quick squeeze.

"Me? Why?"

"Most of my exhaustion is from making myself feel like D'Arcy," he said, glancing away. For an instant, he seemed to have forgotten Shelley completely. A film of coldness clouded his aquamarine eyes, and a shudder rippled up her spine to the nape of her neck. "That character you created is a real son of a—"

"I know all about it," she interrupted, reaching forward to place her hand on his lips to still the flow of his words. Even his voice, she noticed, was different, almost as though he had become the character. "I've been watching you, though, and you seem to have grasped his moodiness. You're really doing a tremendous job— even with a bad script!" she added with a twinkle.

"You're only saying that because it's true," he said with a grin, his normal good nature returning at once. "Now, about that tour . . ."

The next day, Shelley boarded the bus loaded with giggling tourists dressed in splashy vacation attire, their eyes hidden behind the regulation Hollywood-style sunglasses. A quick glance at her companions made her feel ill at ease, but with her pen and a notepad tucked in her shoulder bag, she was prepared to make the most of the drive through Beverly Hills. Listening to the monotonous drone of the guide's voice through the hand-held microphone, she kept her eyes fixed on the sights that brought oohs and ahs to the lips of her fellow tourists. Soon her writer's imagination surfaced and she found herself actually interested in the houses, whose architecture ranged from Spanish to Italian to Oriental. The stories about the estates revealed interesting insights about their owners, and her pen scratched hurriedly over her notepad. Pages of notes rolled over the spiral binding as she jotted down observations that would one day be used to create characters for a new novel.

As the bus cruised down Rodeo Drive, Shelley found her attention wandering from the opulent shops and centering again on David, wondering about his California home and why he had chosen not to buy a home in Beverly Hills. He had said he was rich, hinted that there had been a time in his life when he had felt a need to impress . . . whom? To Shelley, it seemed that an address in Beverly Hills would have been sufficient to achieve his goal.

Consumed with curiosity about David, she saw little of the splendor unfolding before her eyes as she continued to speculate about the man who was still a mystery to her. The home he had invited her to stay at on the fringes of a state park he referred to as his retreat, and the apartment he kept in New York was for whenever he was lucky enough to find work on Broadway. But he called Rehoboth Beach "home base."

Her reflections moved on as she tried to visualize the home she had been invited to use if she moved north with the film company. Would it be a true retreat, off the beaten track, as remote as David's home at Rehoboth Beach?

On the way back to her hotel after the tour, Shelley recalled Darby's thoughtful remark: "You two have so much in common . . ." Was it possible, she wondered, that she and David were, indeed, alike? The more she learned of David, the more she realized that he, like she, preferred isolation and privacy in order to pursue their uncommon interests. But, she argued with herself, David was a successful movie star, a man who should thrive on public acclaim. He certainly had a number of friends, too many to qualify himself as a recluse. She recalled that Chris had surrounded himself with people he claimed were friends, but Shelley had soon learned that they were only associates, people who were drawn to the actor because of his profession. David's friends, she had come to realize from close observation, were true friends, people who cared about him, respected him, like Laura London, Vittorio Spellini and a host of others.

Caught up in the many facets of David's personality, comparing it with her own, Shelley walked through her days in a trance without being aware of what was going on about her. No matter where she was or what she was doing, always in the back of her mind was David Warren, and as the days became weeks, she began to look forward to seeing his California home.

When the entire cast and crew headed north to

the cypress groves of Carmel, Shelley traveled with them. When they arrived at the site, where curious pelicans, cormorants, sea lions and otters cast baleful glances at the gypsy troup invading their rocky terrain, she could not disguise her delight with the wildlife. Climbing up the sandstone cliffs with the agility of a teenager, she marveled at the gnarled Monterey cypresses sculpted by the wind as they bent to meet the boisterous sea. Every view was like a classic photograph miraculously come to life just for her to enjoy. Caught up in the enchantment of the area, she forgot her worries about the upcoming meeting with the studio bosses, which had finally been arranged.

Even her concern and apprehension regarding David seemed to recede to a dark and seldom-used corner of her mind, so that she offered no argument when he insisted upon driving her to his home on the outskirts of Point Lobos. As they drove, she gazed raptly at the slashing surf crashing against the shoreline. Gentle trails wandered through fragrant woods, offering her small peeks into the rocky coves beyond. Breathing in the fresh scent of wild iris, the heady fragrance of sage mingling with lilac, she stored up impressions of the enchanted landscape. Intoxicated with its rare beauty, she was oblivious to everything, even to David, who drove slowly, expertly, silently, allowing her to drink her fill of the heady atmosphere.

When they pulled up before a tall sandstone wall with iron gates, Shelley came to herself. Glancing right and left, she saw no sign of any people. As they drove through the towering gates and along a winding dirt road, she spied the look of pride suffusing David's face and realized that this was part of his home and an extension of the wildlife preserve.

Just when she was beginning to think there were no buildings, no house, David swung the car in a circle and announced, "Your new home!"

Bewildered, Shelley swiveled her head. Narrowing her eyes against the bright sun, she spied the outline of a slanting roof jutting from the granite rocks to her right. Beneath the roof was what appeared to be a sizable cabin constructed solely of sandstone and glass, and surrounded by carefully shaped cypresses that provided a natural canopy for the ground cover of bright flowers.

"Oh, it's beautiful!" she breathed. "David, how can you tear yourself away from this spot?"

Turning her attention to him, she saw his lips were curved in a smile, but she could see nothing of his eyes behind their mirrored sunglasses. Boldly, she reached out and whipped the glasses from his nose.

"Why do you wear those things all the time?" she said, clicking them onto the dashboard. "Everybody in California seems to be addicted to them!"

He laughed good-naturedly. "There's a good reason for it, too, at least for those of us in the movie business. Because of the hours we work, we look like hell without our makeup or shades."

Shelley studied him, observed his perfect features, noted the bronze tone of his skin that emphasized the brilliance of his glittering blue green eyes and felt a familiar stirring in her heart. He did look tired, she noticed, her glance resting briefly on the shadows beneath his eyes, the weary lines etched each side of his mouth. Still, he was undoubtedly the most attractive man she had ever known. But she wasn't about to admit that to him and feed his ego. Distressed by the direction her thoughts had taken, she laughed gently and glanced away.

"Talk about women and their vanity!" she remarked dryly. "There's no vanity like an actor's, is there?" Recognizing the bitterness of the comment, she sought to make amends by smiling mischievously as she said, "Now, with makeup, you're absolutely devastating. But I don't think you should take to wearing pancake in the bright light of day, even if it does mask your imperfections."

"So you think I'm devastating when I'm made up for the camera, do you?" he said. He leaned toward her, his grin positively devilish, and she realized he was teasing her. "Tell me about my imperfections."

"I'll let you stew about those for a while," she said with impish lightness, something in her making her unwilling to go along with his flirtatious mood. "Are we going to sit here admiring your hill house from a distance, or shall we take a closer look?" she asked when she caught the gleam flaming in his eyes.

Sighing resignedly, he said, "I suppose we'd better go inside and get you settled."

David got out of the car and stretched as if he were truly exhausted from the drive. Coming around to her side of the car, he opened the door and placed his hand lightly beneath her elbow.

She swung her legs until her feet touched the gravel drive. His touch contained so much electricity that Shelley found herself holding her breath lest he discover the degree of emotion his warm fingers had stirred within her.

"You know that Harley and Carlo will be coming by later, don't you?" he asked, reminding her that an informal meeting between the studio executives had finally been arranged. She was to meet with the script director and the associate producer of the film, who had agreed to come to this hushed spot. "I thought you'd be more relaxed here. It's more comfortable than those studio boardrooms, and I'm hoping you won't let them intimidate you. Remember, at the studio they have the upper hand, but for now I want you to regard this as your home. As far as they're concerned, it is."

"Thank you for thinking of that," Shelley murmured, her voice trembling as a wave of warmth suffused her cheeks. Averting her eyes, she cast an appreciative glance over the sun-dappled landscape and longed to believe he meant what he had said. Even if he hadn't been sincere, what he said made her achingly aware that she and David were to share this lovely setting as if they were truly enjoying a close relationship.

While he collected her luggage and brought it to the tiled patio entrance, she observed him surreptitiously, admiring his grace, and wished she could turn back the clock, revive their old passions, have another chance to overcome her doubts and distrust and perhaps win his love.

She wondered if Harley Williams and Carlo Mendoza believed that she and David were an item; it was conceivable that outsiders would take the two of them for lovers. During the first days of her Hollywood visit, she and David had spent hours and hours together, and now, with David's home as the setting for the conference, there was no telling what interpretation the executives would give to her relationship with the superstar. Did it matter?

Before she could resolve her ruminations, the hushed silence was interrupted by the excited yapping of dogs. Beset by great paws thumping at her legs, wet tongues licking at her hands, she recognized Fritz and Karl dancing about her with canine delight. Eagerly, she bent to caress their gleaming black heads with genuine pleasure.

"They remember me!" she cried.

"Sure, they do," David drawled, observing the display of mutual affection. "I don't see them coming to welcome me."

"Go to David," she urged Karl, whose gold brown eyes worshiped Shelley. "Go on, both of you! Your master has come home. Let him know you're glad to see him."

Whimpering, the Dobermans turned to David, who hunkered down beside them and began to wrestle with the sleek animals in the manner of a child reunited with his favorite playmates.

"I didn't know you could do that with guard dogs," Shelley remarked.

Peering around Fritz's nuzzling head, David laughed heartily. "A stranger couldn't," he informed her. "Not with these two, believe me."

Watching the trio, Shelley felt her heart swell until it threatened to burst. It's like coming home, she mused wistfully, wishing it could be true. Why was she attracted to men whose most important interest was themselves? Were David not so preoccupied with himself and his career, there might still be a chance for them, she reflected. Then again, perhaps there was a way she could make dreams reality. It was worth a try, she reasoned. This might be a heaven-sent opportunity to make a new start; maybe it wasn't too late for them to discover how much they had in common and come to a workable compromise. Assuming she could accept David's indifference, she might yet convince him to offer a semblance of love. It wasn't what she wanted, but it was better than nothing, better than the aching emptiness she had experienced in the past weeks, an emptiness she now realized only David could fill.

Chapter Thirteen

Shelley found David's house to be a delightfully luxurious retreat. Its spacious rooms were sparsely furnished and decorated in earth tones to create an illusion of living outdoors. The room he had assigned to her was restful, done in warm greens to blend with the lush landscape outside its glass wall, which fronted onto a woodland where pine scented the air. After acquainting herself with its sumptuous furnishings, she showered and took a nap, awakening refreshed and ready to meet with Harley Williams and Carlo Mendoza, who were waiting in the inviting den at the rear of the ground floor.

David had thoughtfully provided iced cocktails to ease the tension and soften the executive hearts of stone. His ploy must have worked, she mused, for when she joined them, she found them laughing amiably and more agreeable than she had anticipated. After making the introductions and taking part in some light conversation, David quietly departed, leaving Shelley to handle the discussion on her own.

Following David's earlier advice, she assumed a pose of serenity as she made her opening statements. Noticing that she had taken them by surprise, she freshened their drinks and told herself this wasn't going to be much different from all those television interviews she had conducted years ago.

Observing them closely, she realized that she would have to be constantly on guard. As the meeting progressed, it became apparent that the two men had decided to present an irritating air of superiority, as if she knew nothing at all; granted, she was unfamiliar with the intricacies of the film world, but she was too intelligent to be intimidated by the overbearing associate producer of *Paradise Unending* or his pudgy companion who headed the stable of studio writers, a man whose oily smiles and hearty laugh did little to mask his devious nature.

"What you're saying," she said firmly, her eyes resting briefly on each of them, "is that it all comes down to money. Because of a limited budget, which you have already gone beyond, you've taken the liberty of changing my plot, squeezed it and compacted it until it's unrecognizable."

Harley shifted uneasily in the soft leather chair. Averting his eyes from Shelley's unblinking gaze, he turned his attention to the ornate ruby on his little finger as if it were suddenly very important, more important than her remarks. With extreme concentration, he began to wiggle the gem so that it caught the light.

Carlo met Shelley's steady gaze head on as he said with tight-lipped seriousness, "That's about it, Ms. Tremayne. As the associate producer, I'm not happy about it because it's my first venture into this sort of thing. I was hoping this would be a quality film, an Academy Award nominee, a nominee for all sorts of awards. I've invested a lot of my own money in the venture, but now I'm told we have to cut corners because we went way over the budget on salaries, costumes, sets . . ."

"How did you spend the money originally allocated?" she asked boldly. "I know some of it was spent on costumes and sets, salaries and so on, but how much actual film was shot other than publicity shots?" Before they could respond, she fired another question at them. "Is any of that film usable?"

Carlo's brows rose as he realized she knew what she was talking about. "We filmed a lot of tight shots of the actors for lighting and camera angles, some dialogue was done, but . . . I suppose it could be spliced into the film, but—"

"But what?" she interrupted. "Don't tell me you don't use tight shots because of wide screens in the theaters, because I know close-ups are still fashionable. The adoring public thrives on every infinitesimal pore of its idols' faces." She watched, delighted, as the men's faces showed their discomfort with the hard-hitting approach she was taking. "Before we get sidetracked and carried away with the pros and cons of camera work, I want to know why my script was abandoned. It was abandoned, wasn't it? In favor of something produced by the studio that might or might not keep costs down after you'd gone over the budget?"

Harley's attention swung from the humongous ruby; he glanced up, his shifty eyes colliding with Shelley's accusing stare. "Ms. Tremayne, you have to realize that we're dealing with a public who wants likable heros, and Lord D'Arcy is not particularly likable. The people who'll come to see this movie are hard-core fans of David Warren and Laura London. After they've seen the movie, we hope they'll be fans of Jenny Sinclair, but we know they'll want to empathize with Davey and Lol, and frankly, they can't do that the way you've written the characters. Your script concentrated on Maryanne as the sole sympathetic character. That won't do."

Refusing to back down, Shelley said, "Are you saying that the people who bought and read my book will welcome a reversal of D'Arcy's character? I think not. I'm positive that many of those who will pay out hard cash to see this film will be familiar with the book and anxious to compare it to the motion picture. As for *Davey* and *Lol*," she added with sarcastic emphasis, "don't you think they deserve a chance to show the public that they can do something besides look pretty and recite lines? They're both established professionals, talented performers who might, as you've already pointed out, become Academy Award nominees if given a chance to use their skills. On that basis alone, I think you could adjust the budget, speed up the schedule or do whatever else might be necessary to cut costs without going too far from the demands of my script."

The glance that passed between Carlo and Harley, combined with their astonished expressions, convinced Shelley that she had made a valid point. Two hours and several cocktails later, she was able to relax in the knowledge that she had scored many points, made a few concessions and obtained their assurances that her script, with a few minor changes, would be restored for the balance of the filming. The alterations she had agreed to, she admitted when relating her success to David, were necessary to inspire sympathy from the audience and, in the long run, greatly strengthened the screenplay, punctuating its dramatic impact without weakening Shelley's original story.

That night, David and Shelley celebrated her first success in the industry. Before a leisurely meal served outdoors beneath a velvet canopy of glittering stars, he toasted her with vintage champagne. They talked quietly as they ate, and afterward they walked hand in hand through the fragrant woods. For Shelley, it was a dreamlike night of shared companionship similar to the evenings they had known at Rehoboth Beach.

With her hand held in David's firm grip, Shelley's reflections turned inward. Her pulse raced in time with the thunderous beat of her heart, and she knew David was aware of her excitement as his thumb advanced to her wrist to trace sensual circles against the sensitive flesh. Casting sidelong glances at her face, David could not mistake the dancing light in her eyes;

her contentment and happiness seemed complete.

"You seem to be adjusting to my world," he murmured, inclining his head toward her so that his lips feathered her hair when he spoke. "Do you think you can ever come to accept it?"

Was it her imagination, or had he meant to say more? she wondered. The question seemed incomplete, as if he had intended to add the simple words "and me?" But Shelley refused to allow herself to be swept away by romantic notions in the starlit night.

"I might be able to accept it if I had a place like this to come to," she heard herself say. Immediately, she regretted voicing the wistful thought, for it sounded as if she were pressing David for some sort of commitment. "I mean, this is a far cry from the babble of Tinseltown, you have to admit. I doubt I could ever adjust to the madness of the film industry full time. I'm afraid that if I tried, I'd only become jaded."

Squeezing her hand with affection, David chuckled. "Do you think I'm jaded? How little you know of me!" he teased. "I thought you knew that I can't always cope with the madness either. Believe it or not, I don't spend much time in Hollywood. No more than I have to, anyway. It's where I work, the same way the Connecticut stockbroker works in an office on Wall Street. Acting is only a job, Shelley."

She breathed in his healthy male scent and grew dizzy from its potency. Was it possible that he was unaffected by the magical sweetness of the night, the closeness of their bodies that found their hips swaying in unison as they walked? Did he feel nothing when his arm brushed against her breast with the swinging motion of their joined hands? Was she alone in experiencing these erotically stimulating sensations?

Forcing a lightness to her voice, she said, "But what a job, David! Wall Street brokers don't make passionate love to Jenny Sinclair for hours on end."

His steps halted, and with a slight tug on her hand he forced Shelley to stop and face him. Tilting her face up to the silver light of the moon, he searched its fine features curiously. "Do I hear a note of jealousy in your voice? It seems to me we've had this conversation before," he murmured quietly. "Are you covetous of my time with Jenny?"

Laughing nervously, Shelley averted her eyes. "It was only a comment, for goodness' sake! How's young Jenny getting along?" Had she actually been so foolish as to reveal her growing jealousy of the lovely young girl who shared David's days, his embraces beneath the hot spotlights under the watchful eye of the camera? "It's hard for an outsider to tell whether or not she's a competent actress. All I've seen her do are those torrid love scenes, but that doesn't tell me if she's proving a good choice for Maryanne."

"Shelley, Shelley," he murmured, gathering her against him in a warm embrace. Rocking her back and forth, he placed his lips against her hair and laughed lightly. "Let me assure you, Jenny and I are not exactly having the time of our lives doing those love scenes. Can you imagine how difficult it is to spend hours leaning on your elbows, worrying about the camera angles, the shadows, the microphone hidden in your armpit, your wig and all the other things that don't show up on the screen? Even Jenny's sweet lips become tiresome after six or seven hours. As for passion, it doesn't come easily if you remember that only a few inches above Jenny's head is a script girl feeding her the lines, while kneeling at my side is a light specialist checking the glints in my beard, the shadow on my nose that makes me look like a pirate. Think about that for a minute. Does it sound romantic?"

Shelley thought about it and chuckled. "Not really. But you still haven't told me what you think of Jenny. Watching the two of you together, it seems as though you're getting along well."

Slowly David allowed his hands to slide up to her neck. He held her face immobile as he said gently, "Jenny is young; she's new to the business and has a lot to learn. I want this film to be outstanding. My ego demands it. So I am willing to spend whatever time it takes to turn Ms. Sinclair into a fairly competent actress. She has trouble learning her lines. I get annoyed by her lack of concentration, but that's why we have a script girl hovering about while we make what you call passionate love for the camera. My interest in Jenny is purely professional, Shelley. Does that satisfy your curiosity?" When Shelley offered no comment, he said in a husky whisper, "To ease your mind and reassure your green-eyed monster, surely you remember that you and I have known some passionate moments in privacy, without script girls or cameras. You haven't forgotten, have you?" he pressed softly.

Confused by his low-voiced question, the warmth of his hands against her cool flesh, the fluttering of her heart, Shelley gazed blankly into his face, studied his classic features that appeared ghostly and unreadable in the rays of the moon.

"Why can't you trust me, Shelley?" he murmured. "Is it my fault that I resemble him? Can't you forgive? Forget? Say something, Shelley. Talk to me. Let me know what's going on in that brain of yours. Do you feel anything for me, or is it all for him? Are you comparing me with him? Or are you just jealous of Jenny?"

Frowning, Shelley tried to free herself of his disturbing grip. What was he saying? Why was he making her think of Chris? Did he honestly believe her heart still belonged to him? After all they had shared, the passion she had exhibited for him, was he so blind as to assume that the gift of herself she had bestowed upon him once and offered again, only to be refused, was a mockery, a meaningless gesture made because he resembled Chris Devon?

"You know I have feelings for you," she said at last, her voice a raspy croak. "I'm grateful for all you've done for me in this script business, and I admire and respect your talent. And I'd be lying if I said I don't enjoy being with you, living in your beautiful home." She longed to pour out her heart to him, but feared being rebuffed again; certain that she couldn't cope with his indifference, she chose to go no further.

"And that's it?" he said, his features distorted

with disbelief. "You don't want me as I want you?"

"Want, David?" she echoed. "Of course I want you. You certainly know that you're a desirable man. I'm not immune to desire. But you know that, don't you?"

"Oh, God, Shelley, I don't understand you at all!" he groaned, releasing her so abruptly that she staggered crazily on legs that were like jelly.

He swung away to pace ahead of her, seemingly oblivious to her presence as he muttered to himself, "I'm weary of being wanted because of *what* I am instead of *who* I am! What I wouldn't give to have someone else's name, another face . . ."

Trailing behind him, Shelley asked, "What are you talking about, David? Have I upset you?"

He spun around, his eyes wild as his hands raked through the thickness of his hair. "Upset me? You? Perish the thought! I asked a simple question—or what seemed simple to me—and I don't even know why I asked it."

"Ask it again, David," Shelley whispered. She needed desperately to hear it again, and she waited breathlessly as he studied her through eyes that were expressionless, devoid of emotion.

"Do you want me, Shelley? Here and now? Or do you want the man I resemble, the man who used you? Is it vengeance you want? Are you using me as the vessel for your bitterness?" His voice was as blank as his handsome features, but his hands were extended toward her in supplication.

Perhaps it was his hands, or maybe the bleakness of his eyes, that brought a lump to her throat and impelled her toward him until her arms reached for him, closed about his muscular physique and pressed him to her softness while her quiet voice murmured, "David, I do want you. Right now, I want you desperately. Only you."

His answer was a muffled moan. With his head buried against her collarbone, he pressed his lips urgently to the throbbing pulse at the base of her arching throat. "If it isn't me you want, don't tell me. Tonight, I don't think I could forgive you for that."

Lifting his head, he hungrily sought her mouth with his. Their lips came together with soul-stirring intensity; tongues searched, found, dueled in a fury of unleashed passion that swept them along on a tidal wave of sensation. With one hand at the small of her back, strong, firm, unbearably persuasive, he moved his other sensuously upward along her spine as the kiss deepened, bonding them immutably together.

Shelley's eager hands explored the hardness of his muscled back, traveled downward to his narrow waist, where they linked briefly before moving on to tease the flesh beneath his fitted slacks. She was achingly aware of the movements of his fingers tantalizing her firm breasts through the flimsy fabric of her dinner dress, and when she felt herself falling backward, she offered no complaint, knowing that he too was drifting toward the damp ground, seeking a more complete union than the mere melding of lips.

Feeling the hard earth beneath her hips, she drew back and breathed, "David, my dress . . ."

"Don't talk, don't say anything," he muttered, his hands working their particular magic on her writhing curves. A cool blast of air swept between them, and she realized that he had managed to free her from the confinement of her clothes. Awash on a surging wave of sensation, she had not been aware of his experienced movements . . . or cared. . . .

Anxiously, she commenced to work at his shirt, fumbling with the buttons, the clasp of his belt, the zipper that resisted her feverish motions but finally fell away in a whisper of sound. Greedily, her hands sought his naked flesh, caressed him into rigid awareness. All the while, his fingers and lips were touching, stroking, licking, igniting fires, coaxing her into pliant submissiveness. Bare flesh touched bare flesh, pleasure radiated outward into the cool night, emotions whirled and eddied, senses shortcircuited. Unable to restrain an outcry of delight, Shelley heard her own voice above the muffled moans coming from David's throat.

"Oh, I do want you!" she sighed, yielding to the searing need that had been building for weeks.

"Oh, my sweet Shelley," he moaned, his tongue tantalizing her nipples into peaks of raw sensitivity under his moist manipulation.

In a symphony of entwined arms and legs, they moved as one, tasting, touching and arousing each other until it seemed there were no more sensations to be experienced. David's fingers stroked the quivering flesh of her inner thighs, bringing a sigh of pure pleasure to her lips. Positioning himself so that he straddled her hips, he replaced his hands with his mouth, rousing her to a state of sensual insanity.

When Shelley could stand no more, she took him by the chin and lifted his face. Mutely, she searched his passion-glazed eyes. Her hands encouraged him to rest his body against hers so that she could trace his hard flanks, run her fingertips up and down his spine with the lightness of feathers until he was totally roused and as eager as she for their consummation.

"Please, David," she coaxed, arching herself toward him in frank invitation. "I'm on fire. If we don't do something soon, I'll burn up!"

"We're going to do something, sweet Shelley," he assured her, taking one last possessive taste of her bruised lips before dropping his head and allowing his bearded face to sweep down the length of her aroused flesh, brush against her swollen nipples, over her belly, along the parted thighs to her bent knees, past the shapely calves and on to her feet. His lips worshiped every inch of her, and when his warm mouth arrived at her toes, he laved them with his tongue, taking each toe into his mouth and tasting its sweetness as if it were the rarest of nectars.

"Oh, David!"

"I'm here, Shelley," he replied, unhurriedly rising up only to lower himself so that his nakedness covered hers, his hardness electrifying as it pulsed against her primed flesh.

Then he was inside her, filling her with his strength, assuaging her hungers with his maleness. With each thrust of his hips, he drove her passion higher and higher. Currents of wild sensation swept them along as they soared as one through the maelstrom of mutual desire and beyond to new realms of unexplored rapture that left them breathless and panting when they at last plummeted back to reality.

Still joined together, they breathed in great gasping gulps while the damp night air whispered over their exhausted bodies. When Shelley would have spoken, David placed a light finger to her lips, shushing her, before he placed his mouth against hers in the ultimate expression of pleasure and contentment. Slowly he removed himself from her body to roll onto his side, one hand cupping his head as he lay gazing up into the vaulted canopy that was the night sky.

Some time later, Shelley turned to look at him. His eyes were closed; he appeared to be sleeping. Raising herself up on one elbow, she leaned over him to study the relaxed lines of his face. The moon had disappeared behind a milky cloud, making it difficult to see his features. Bending closer, she brushed the tips of her sensitive breasts against his chest and elicited an instant response from him. One muscular arm circled her shoulders; a strong-fingered hand traced the curve of her jaw.

"You are so beautiful, Shelley," he whispered.

"You make me feel beautiful," she replied just as softly.

"We were beautiful together, hm?" he suggested with a hint of a smile. "I've always wondered what it would be like to make love beneath the stars, out in the open like this."

"Me too," she confessed shyly, dropping her head to plant a light kiss to his still-parted lips. "It's like magic, isn't it? Just us and the stars. Of course, the moon does resemble a spotlight," she teased, glancing around with mock anxiety. "Where's the script girl?"

"I gave her the night off, so you're on your own," he growled, his arms gripping her so that she lay atop him, her breasts flattened against his rock-hard chest, her hips resting with almost painful intimacy against his newly aroused manhood. "This night is ours and we'll make our own dialogue, okay?"

"Who needs dialogue?" she murmured, placing her lips to his.

At the same time that his tongue flicked at her mouth, demanding entry, his hips arched and he thrust himself hungrily into her. Clinging to him, she allowed herself to be spun in a slow circle until she was once again beneath him. Winding her arms and legs about his heaving physique, she sought an even closer union. Almost immediately, she felt his maleness pulsing deep within her as she moved out of herself to soar with him above the damp earth, above the whispering treetops. One thought blazed in her consciousness as they crested at the apex of their rapture: this was no mere man but an extension of herself, a part of her, a part she could never live without. Before she could consider the significance of her discovery, they crashed into the erotic galaxy where shimmering shards of light exploded all around them, searing their fused flesh.

It was nearly dawn when they returned to the

darkened house. Arms wound around each other, they entered through the sliding glass doors at the back of the house. Pausing, they glanced wistfully back at the night that was all too quickly turning to day.

"In a few hours, I have to leave," David murmured.

"Leave?" she echoed, her glance cutting to his.

"I'm afraid so," he said, dejection marring the perfection of his features. "We're going to be putting in long days on location. The studio has given me a trailer for the duration, but it's not like this. You're not there," he whispered. "Will you be afraid to stay here alone? You won't really be alone, you know," he said quickly when he saw her disappointment. "I have servants hidden all over the place."

Forcing a laugh to mask her disappointment, Shelley admitted that she had noticed the houseboy and heard muffled voices coming from the direction of the kitchen. "Am I permitted to socialize with them? Say things like good morning, thank you and so forth?"

"You have my permission to say whatever you please. I haven't beaten them lately, so they may be getting soft and will welcome your kindness," he replied, imitating her mock-serious tone. "I hope you'll continue coming to the set."

"Don't tell me you need my moral support? That you won't be able to function without me?" she teased, realizing that she would come as faithfully as an old dog trailing its master.

Shaking her shoulders affectionately, he grinned down into her upturned face. "Something like that. I've come to look forward to seeing you standing on the sidelines, and I'd miss you if you stopped coming," he admitted.

"Then I'll find time to be there," she said with a smile, giving in to a glowing sense of being needed. "Are you sure you wouldn't rather emote without my critical presence?"

"Don't you mean 'make love to Jenny' rather than 'emote'?" he teased. "I hate to be the one to tell you this, but we've still got a lot of those love scenes to film before we get to the serious emoting."

Pursing her lips, Shelley pretended to be considering this for a moment. "I'll just have to endure it somehow, then, won't I?"

Even as she spoke lightly, she knew it wasn't going to be easy to stand silently by, observing the man she loved in the steamy embrace of another, much younger woman. At that moment, she could not conceive of a greater pain.

Chapter Fourteen

As the days raced by, Shelley's visits to the filming area became less and less frequent. Though at first she told herself she was there to observe the mechanics of moviemaking, she eventually had to acknowledge that the daily treks were a means of being near David. As the shooting schedule accelerated until the crew was keeping frantic predawn-to-midnight hours, she became aware of two startling developments. First of all, she could not avoid noticing that David was becoming more and more oblivious to her presence, unaware of her as a person. At the same time, she became aware of an eerie change in his personality. It wasn't just a trick of makeup and lighting, as she at first suspected, but a frightening metamorphosis that altered not only his features, but his character, his very spirit. Consumed by the character he was portraying, David had somehow managed to actually become Lord Andrew D'Arcy.

Even in those fleeting moments when he was free to be with her for a quick lunch, the infrequent times when he was ordered to take a much-needed break, Shelley noticed that David's eyes darted anxiously, his lips twitched nervously and his hands moved continuously, as if he feared losing the character if he relaxed his guard while away from the camera.

Resolving to avoid contact with David, but unable to stay away from him completely, she admitted only to a fascination with the business of shooting a movie on location. Telling herself there was no harm in observing and learning, she continued to visit the shooting site but always managed to stand unobtrusively to one side, unnoticed by David, and completely hypnotized by his abilities and his uncanny behavior patterns that raised questions in her mind.

"Damn, he's good, isn't he?"

The hushed comment caught Shelley's attention. Glancing away from the tense action being filmed a few yards distant, she met the admiring glance of Laura London. The glamorous star was almost unrecognizable in her stragglyhaired wig, her delicate complexion disguised with dark makeup. To anyone unaware of her part in the film, she might have been a gypsy fortune-teller who had wandered onto the closed set.

"He's good, isn't he?" Laura repeated, her smile the grotesque grin of Angelique, a character plucked from Shelley's imagination but brought to life by the talented actress. "I knew he was capable of doing the part, but I never dreamed he'd be so magnificent!" she enthused, grabbing hold of Shelley's arm and squeezing it as she was caught up in the scene they were watching.

"He's too good," Shelley murmured, her attention drawn again to the tense interaction between Maryanne and D'Arcy. "I feel like a Peeping Tom."

Laura laughed, the sound low and husky. "Davey's done a good coaching job on Jenny, wouldn't you say? She came to us an inexperienced ingenue, but she'll go away an accomplished actress."

"He's done an even better job on himself," Shelley commented quietly. "He's become so heartless and cruel, I don't even like him."

"You're not supposed to!" chuckled Laura. "You wrote the dialogue, established D'Arcy's character, so you of all people ought to know he's not your endearing boy next door."

"Yes, I did, didn't I?" Shelley's words were thoughtful, her expression blank. She continued to observe the angry confrontation being filmed, but her reflections were far away and deeply disturbing as she pondered the strange behavior of the man she had begun to believe she loved.

"You should be proud of this film, Shelley, dear. I just hope you're prepared for the notoriety it's going to get," Laura said.

"Notoriety?" echoed Shelley absently. "Oh, you mean all the hype about Jenny and David? It's all publicity, you know. There's nothing to it." Her words sounded hollow to her ears as she struggled to convince herself that there was no romance budding off screen between the two performers, that the sensational journalism centered around Jenny and David was nothing more than fabrication to generate interest in the movie.

Laura grunted irritably. "I'm not talking about the stories going the rounds. The media always play up an attractive couple making love for the camera. The whole world loves a lover, and it draws attention to the movie. You get used to it. What I'm talking about are the rumors flying that all of us will be reaping awards, including you."

"Me? Why?"

"Ever heard of Best Screenplay? You're sure to be in line for it, my dear." Laura's normally sexy voice had dropped to a whisper, her lips close to Shelley's ear. "I think the turning point was in the choice of Davey Warren. He's so professional and so determined to make this a quality picture, we all try harder just to measure up to his greatness."

Shelley turned to study Laura. "He inspires that sort of response in his fellow actors?" she asked.

"You bet he does. He's not just a pretty face." Laura sighed wistfully, adding, "Of course, his face helps, don't you agree? And that marvelous body!"

Remembering just how marvelous his body was and the exciting things David could do with it, Shelley glanced away. "There are lots of pretty faces and marvelous bodies in this business," she commented.

"Yep, there sure are," agreed Laura. "But very

few of them have Davey's unselfish temperament and personality. He really cares about people, you know, and he cares about our business."

"Unselfish?" Shelley echoed stupidly. "He cares?" she asked doubtfully.

"Sure he does. He looks out for those he cares about, too. How about the way he went to bat for you? Doesn't that tell you how much he cares?"

He cares about the script, his lines, his precious image, Shelley argued silently, unable to agree with Laura's simple statements. People mean nothing to him unless they can be used as stepping stones, she went on mutely. I mean nothing to him other than as a writer who wrote good lines for him to speak, a body to slake his desire, an ear to listen to his opinionated bragging . . .

"Davey has worked hard to get where he is," Laura was saying in her conspiratorial whisper. "It hasn't come easy, you can be sure. For years, he was used by the studio bosses who wanted to make a few fast bucks from his good looks and popularity. They arranged his life, even told him which women to see and which not to be seen with. He couldn't make a move without criticism. I heard he once wanted to marry a nice girl but the studio nixed it. Thank God, times have changed, but until you came along, Davey didn't mingle much. He was more or less a lone wolf." Laura chuckled merrily. "Although 'wolf' isn't quite the right word; if there's one thing Davey Warren isn't, it's a wolf. He's a true gentleman, maybe the last of the breed." Again she sighed wistfully. "If only I were ten, fifteen years younger, I'd put a dent in his heart, believe me. Of course, I'll bet you could teach me about denting his heart, couldn't you, dear?"

Shelley might have been encouraged by Laura's reflections, but she was no longer listening. The director had shouted "Cut!" and as the company began to move aimlessly about the cypress grove, Shelley's eyes had fixed on David. He paced restlessly, a cup of steaming coffee clutched in his sunbrowned hand. At his side was Jenny, her sweetly attractive face tilted up to his. Deep in conversation, they appeared oblivious to the others milling about.

Not wanting to interrupt their animated conversation, and mindful of her resolve to stay away from David and his erratic behavior, Shelley mumbled something she hoped was polite to Laura, who cast her a curious glance before cutting her eyes to David once more.

"You're not leaving already, are you?" Laura asked, her quick footsteps bringing her alongside Shelley, who was rapidly retreating from the shooting site. "We're only taking a break because Jenny forgot her lines again. We'll resume shooting in a minute."

"I realize that," Shelley said, masking her disappointment that David had not made an excuse to be with her while Jenny Sinclair reviewed her lines. "I have some errands to do before I go back to the house. No sense in making two trips into Carmel," she added with a forced smile.

"Any word for Davey?" pressed Laura. "I mean, he'll wonder where you've gone."

"I doubt he'll even notice I'm not here," Shelley said with feigned lightness. "If he does, he knows where to find me."

Heading for the parking lot, Shelley told herself she hadn't lied; she did have errands. She wanted to find a stationery shop, purchase a ream of paper and get started on the new novel she had been considering for the past weeks. With so much time on her hands, she saw no reason why she should put off drafting the new and considerably brighter story that had formed in her imagination and sometimes eased her aching heart and mind.

Rounding the gate separating the shooting site from the busy area reserved for mobile dressing rooms, she considered going to David's trailer. It might be nice to wait there in the cool air conditioning, fix him a light meal that they could enjoy when he returned at the end of the day. But no, she decided, he wouldn't want that; her presence might even be resented by the hard man he had recently become. Resolutely, she swung away, her steps quickening as she approached the parking lot.

Shelley almost missed seeing the man standing in the shadows beside a shiny travel trailer, his alert black eyes following her movements with bemused interest, but when her glance swung back again toward the crowd gathered around the cameras, she met his bright gaze head on. For a moment, she was sure she was hallucinating. Her eyes darted anxiously to the cypress grove, where David and Jenny sat huddled together, their heads turned away from her.

If it wasn't David—and obviously it wasn't—then it had to be . . .

"Shelley? Long time no see!"

Frozen to the spot, she stared disbelievingly as he swaggered toward her, a beguiling smile pasted on his lips.

"So you've come out of hiding," he remarked as he drew near, his strides assured and so like those adopted by David in his portrayal of Lord D'Arcy. "You're looking great. Success agrees with you." He halted directly before her, his grin widening flirtatiously. "Well, say something. 'Hello, how are you?' is always a good start."

"Hello, Chris," she said with numb lips. "How are you?"

"Great. Never better."

"What are you doing here?"

"I work here, haven't you heard? Got a call from my agent saying I'd been specifically requested for a bit part in this epic. Of course, it's smaller than I'd like it to be, but if I play my cards right, it can be a good opportunity for me. At least I'm having the experience of working with the great David Warren," he said with a touch of envy.

His insidious remark caused her to realize that, with Chris in the cast, David had been studying his mannerisms, his speech patterns, adopting his subtlety . . . his malice . . .

"Who knows?" Chris was saying optimistically, "I may be so believable, the writers will expand my part so I'll be in the running for one of those awards everybody is tasting."

He hasn't changed a bit, she mused. Still padding his small parts, convincing himself that he's the next big star and trying to convince everybody else of it as well.

Collecting her wits, Shelley swallowed and said in her best deadpan, "I wouldn't count on the writers, Chris. As one well acquainted with the script crew, I've found that the original author is a hard nut to crack and not easily swayed by mediocre actors doing walk-ons."

She had actually done it! She had asserted herself with Christopher Devon, made a small down payment on the sizable mortgage he had long ago put on her fragile ego. Having made a start, she felt that future payments would be much less painful.

"Which part are you doing?" she asked, sorting through her mental files in an effort to pinpoint his character.

"Joshua, D'Arcy's older brother," he replied, his cockiness fading as the significance of her remark sank in. "Like I said, it's small, and I'm a bit young for it, but the makeup crew does its best to age me."

"Oh, so you're in makeup now, but not in costume," she said cuttingly, fully aware that he was in neither. How easy it was now to find his flaws, to stab at his fragile vanity as he had delighted in doing to her for so long.

He scowled at her before flashing his twisted grin. "You haven't changed much, Shel. Still scoring points, kidding around, aren't you?"

Ignoring the hurt in his once-vibrant voice, she asked with casual interest, "How's the wife? Any kids?"

His gray-streaked black head lowered; the frown knitting his brow deepened. "I thought you knew," he mumbled. "She divorced me a year ago. Convinced the court I was sponging off her millions, using her family connections to further myself."

"I wonder what made her think that?" Shelley made no attempt to smother her sarcasm. "And you such a big star and so busy! I'm surprised the courts bought her story." She knew the comment hurt because, other than a minor part in a recent Broadway play, she couldn't remember reading any reports of his work.

After casting a quizzical glance at her deadpan expression, he straightened and said, "Let's talk about you. From what I hear, your career has really taken off. Your book was a big success, and now this film—"

"You've read my book, then?" Had he recognized himself in D'Arcy? Recognized Maryanne?

"Uh, no, you know me, Shel, I'm not much of a reader. I never read heavy stuff, books and the like, but I talk to the right people and devour the trade papers. Your star is shining everywhere." Rocking smugly on his heels, he added, "I knew you'd find yourself one day."

"Find myself?"

"Yeah. I knew you were capable of great things, greater than that talk show you had. And I was right, wasn't I? You're raking in the big money now, I'll bet."

"I'm not worrying about paying the rent," she replied curtly, adding, "or letting anyone else pay it for me." She was hardly surprised that he was impressed by her financial success.

"That was a low blow, Shel," he said in a wounded tone. "We both paid our own way. We had an agreement, remember?"

"I remember." How she wished she could forget their agreement to share expenses and live together while pursuing separate lifestyles! "If you'll excuse me, I must be going," she said, making a move to pass him, but she was stopped by his restraining hand on her arm.

"Don't rush off, Shel," he pleaded in his lowest, most sexy voice, one that once would have tugged at her heart but now left her cold. "Where are you staying, in case we get the chance to be together for old times' sake?"

"You don't want to see me, Chris," she snapped, pulling free of his grip.

He studied her for a silent moment before saying, "If I know you, that translates to, you don't want to see me."

"You always were a bright fellow!"

"Oh, Shelley, love, I don't think you know what you're saying. We go back a long way. Remember the good times we had in the old days?" Again, he clasped her arm to run his fingers with sensual lightness over the soft bare skin exposed by her sleeveless blouse. "I know I want to see you, be with you again," he crooned huskily. "Tell me where you're staying, where I can get in touch with you."

As if hypnotized, she stared at the tanned fingers circling her upper arm. Where was the magic those fingers could work on her during her years of yearning? Aloud, she said, "I'm staying at a friend's house near Point Lobos."

As if he had been seared by tongues of fire, Chris withdrew his hand and whistled appreciatively. "David Warren has a place up that way. Is that where you're staying?" His accusing eyes impaled her. "And after that nasty crack about somebody else paying your rent! Is property ownership what you look for now that your tastes have matured?" His insolent lips spread in a malicious smile.

Shelley's brows rose. One hand lifted. When a cracking sound echoed in her ears, she realized that she had actually slapped his square jaw. A sense of triumph swept over her as she spun away from him to stalk to the parking lot.

Unlocking the door of David's car, she braved a backward glance and was rewarded with the sight of Chris's stunned face, his mouth gaping and his dark eyes wide with shock.

Shelley was absorbed in drafting a rough outline of the second chapter of her new novel when she became aware of the agitated barking of Fritz and Karl. Certain David had come home after three weeks on the set, she recalled his last visit. Their conversation had been stilted, and she had marveled at the mannerisms he had adopted, which were so uncannily similar to those of Chris Devon. She had wondered if the two men had become close since being thrown together by the tight shooting schedule. Assuming they had become friends, she had held herself aloof from David's eager attempts at lovemaking, sent him away frustrated and irritable.

When the barking grew more insistent, she turned down the volume on the stereo system before cautiously stepping through the sliding doors into the moonlit garden.

"David? Is it you?" she called.

When there was no response, she hastened back through the sliding doors and pulled them shut. Outside, Fritz and Karl were still yelping. The cries were not those of welcome; it was not David returning unexpectedly. A stranger had ventured onto the private property, she realized as the barking increased until it was deafening, frightening in its intensity.

Until now, she had never experienced any fear, even when she knew the servants had gone to their cottages, situated some distance from the house. Purposefully, she walked to the telephone and placed her hand on the receiver. Should she call the police?

"Shelley! Call off the damned dogs!"

For an instant, she was sure the voice was David's, but when she would have darted into the night, eager to greet him, she recalled another man whose voice was deceptively similar, a man who would think nothing of invading another's estate if there was something there . . . or someone . . . he thought he wanted.

"You're not welcome here, Chris!" she shouted angrily.

"Shelley!" Chris's voice was now an anguished moan. "Call off these damned dogs before they tear me apart!"

Bravely, she stepped out into the moonlit night. Haloed by the bright lights of the house, she followed the brick path until she was swathed in inky darkness. Spying Chris's ashen face only a few yards distant, she gazed in horror at the sight of the dogs circling his trembling frame, their fangs bared in warning. Remembering David's warning that only he could roughhouse with the guard dogs, she stepped briskly forward.

"Here, boys!" Was that calm voice hers? she wondered. "Come, Karl! Fritz, no! Sit! Stay!"

Confused, the Dobermans did not immediately comply. Their glittering eyes swung to Shelley. Then, whining a low canine duet, the dogs sat back on their haunches before the man whose wild eyes darted anxiously from them to Shelley.

Narrowing his jet black eyes, Chris studied her. "Are they your dogs?"

"No."

"But they obey you."

"Yes."

"They're Warren's." It was a defeated statement rather than a question. Sighing resignedly, he muttered, "You were always terrified of dogs, any dogs. Yet these two vicious beasts could eat out of your hand, couldn't they?"

"I honestly don't know. I've never tried to feed them."

"But I'll bet you'd like to feed me to them right now, wouldn't you?"

"Sadism isn't my style," she snapped.

"Still the tenderhearted farm girl from Michigan?"

His taunt struck a nerve. "What if I am?" she

replied defensively. "A tender heart is nothing to be ashamed of, I've discovered. What are you doing here, Chris?" she asked. "You weren't invited."

"Since the great David Warren was otherwise occupied, it seemed like a good time to call on my girl, surprise her. You are surprised, aren't you, Shel?"

"I'm not your girl, but I am surprised. Come on, Chris, tell me why you've come here."

"I wanted to see you, be with you."

"Why?"

He grinned and swung closer to her. "Hey, honey, it's me, Chris. We used to have a lot going for us. It was too hot not to cool down. With a little effort, we could rekindle that old flame."

"I'm not interested in rekindling flames, Chris."

"What's wrong, honey? Don't you remember what it was like between us?" His voice cajoled, coaxed, but his eyes slanted cautiously toward the dogs who lay quietly observing the two of them. Eagerly, he reached for her, his hands circling her small waist. "It's been a long time since I held you and kissed you. A man develops a terrible thirst when he goes too long without a drink."

"Don't, Chris!" she warned, stepping backward out of his light embrace. "Listen, you'll find somebody else one day," she assured him. "You always do, don't you? Besides, I don't really earn enough to satisfy your needs."

"Shelley, don't . . . ," he began.

The moonlight illuminated his tortured features, and she knew she had gone too far in a useless effort at hurting him as she had once been hurt. Wanting to make amends, she leaned toward him. "You will find somebody someday, Chris, someone you can love, really love. But it isn't me you want or need."

When she saw the flicker of hope that danced in his eyes, she realized she had soothed his damaged ego and grew embarrassed. Lowering her eyes, she noticed that the Dobermans had come to lie at her feet, their golden eyes worshiping her. She leaned down and tenderly stroked Fritz's sleek cropped ears.

Following her movement, Chris snorted. "I can't believe my eyes. But I'm beginning to understand a few things," he added reflectively. "It's him, isn't it?"

"Him?"

"Warren. You're living here, surrounded by his dogs and his possessions. I suppose you think he loves you. Don't count on it, babe! I've learned a lot about him, let me tell you—"

"Get out, Chris," Shelley interrupted before he could say more. Fearing what he might say, she could not allow him to speak. "I'm not interested in what you think you know or what you have to say."

Disbelief stamped on his features, Chris's eyes held Shelley's. After a moment, he shrugged and muttered, "I'm leaving." When he was almost beyond her range of vision, he swung around and called out, "You may have found yourself, but you've never been very good at picking men, have you, Shel? Good luck with this one. He's a real loner, and loners are users. They like their solitude and don't get attached to women—or haven't you heard?"

"Goodbye, Chris," she replied absently.

Long after he had disappeared into the night, Shelley stood gazing sightlessly into the darkness, wishing she had allowed Chris to say his piece. He seemed to think he knew something about David that could be important to her future.

"What future?" she grumbled aloud. Stooping to Fritz and Karl lying at her feet, she gratefully nuzzled their sleek heads. "Who would have ever thought I'd be more frightened of Chris Devon than of you?" she whispered, and received flicking kisses from their tongues in happy reply.

Straightening, she made her way back to the house. At her side, the dogs kept vigil, their heads swinging from right to left as they searched the area. When she entered the brightly lighted study, they were still marching along beside her.

"Are you fellows allowed in the house?" she asked. Answering her own question, she said, "Why not? Who's here to complain?"

Her eyes swept the comfortable room. This house had been home to her for a while, a place that had offered the peace and quiet she needed to pursue her writing. "I really love this place," she told the dogs. "I'll miss it, but I think it's time to fold my tent and silently steal away. I don't think I want to be here when David decides to come home again. I'd like to think he'll be disappointed, but I guess that's asking too much."

Crossing to the roomy leather wing chair, she was unprepared for the weary male voice that echoed in the midnight silence. "I don't know about being disappointed, but I'd be downright offended by your bad manners and ingratitude! But if you're determined to chase after your dream lover, don't let me stop you!"

Chapter Fifteen

David!" Shelley exclaimed. Rising to a half-crouch, she peered at the man who had silently entered the room. How long had he been home? she wondered. Had he stood in the garden, heard the angry words between herself and Chris? Had he mistaken her attempts at patience for acceptance of Chris's lovemaking?

Slowly, never taking her eyes from his unsmiling face, she lowered herself until she sat stiffly on the edge of the chair. Dazed by the confused mixture of emotions washing over her, she was unaware of the weariness marring his features, did not even notice that the beard that was an integral part of his character for the filming was missing, leaving his square chin clean-shaven, pale and youthfully vulnerable. She saw only an uncommonly attractive face that resembled

Christopher Devon's, a face that revived her bitterness and animosity.

In that hushed heart-stopping moment, Shelley experienced a rush of undiluted hatred that swept aside all other feelings.

Questions scrambled through her consciousness, demanded answers where there were none. Had she truly known tenderness for this man with his too-handsome face? she raged in flaming silence. Had she actually shared with him her deepest, most private thoughts? Fantasized a future with him? Yearned to wrest from him words of love and commitment?

When she would have angrily ordered him from the house, Shelley remembered that this was his home and she was the ungrateful guest who had planned to leave as quietly and quickly as possible. Averting her face from his unblinking gaze, she struggled for composure, sorted through her mind for words that would be politely casual, phrases that would mask the fear and anger permeating her entire being.

"Welcome home," she said, dismayed by the trembling falsetto that bore little resemblance to her normal voice. "Have you eaten? It's late, but if you haven't, I'll fix you something."

How idiotic! she reprimanded herself. Here they stood glaring at each other, each of them boiling with unspoken emotions, and she was offering him supper! His expression revealed his own disappointment with her foolish suggestion.

Clearing her throat, she tried again. "I wish I'd known you were coming home tonight."

"Would it have mattered?" he drawled.

Without replying to the emotionless question, Shelley proceeded to bombard him with her own meaningless interrogation. "Has the shooting schedule been changed? Or is this just a break for you? Oh! Your beard! It's gone! Why?"

David grunted impatiently. "It was bothering me, so I decided to shave it off. I don't need it now."

"You don't need it?" she repeated, the significance of his comment eluding her.

"I'm finished with D'Arcy for a while. There may be retakes later, but for any shooting involving me, I'll let the makeup man supply the beard," he replied curtly.

Still, Shelley did not comprehend the significance of his explanation. Shrugging to cover the awkward moment, she asked with forced nonchalance, "Have you been here long? I mean—"

"I know what you mean, Shelley," he interrupted hoarsely. "I saw Chris leave. I hope he didn't run off because of me. Have you been seeing him while I've been busy on the set?"

Opening her mouth to voice an indignant retort, Shelley found herself groping for words, stammering as she struggled with her tormented emotions. "I . . . ah . . . no, he didn't run off because of you. I didn't know you'd come home, and I'm certain he didn't know either. I don't think it's any of your business, but no, I haven't been seeing him. I ran into him by accident several weeks ago. His sudden visit tonight came as a surprise." In her unreasonable anger at David's abrupt questions, his coldness, she giggled foolishly and despised herself for exhibiting such a glaring lack of poise. "Fritz and Karl didn't want to let him get near the house."

"Oh?"

"They definitely didn't like him. In fact, they would have torn him limb from limb."

"Did they attack?" David asked anxiously.

"No, I intervened and called them off, but I think they made a lasting impression on him. He's as afraid of Dobermans as I was once, so he was pretty scared." Her words came tumbling out in an excited rush of sound.

"If you didn't invite him, why did he come here?" The cold question found Shelley unprepared, unable to dissemble.

"He seemed to think I'd be willing to take up where we left off," she said crisply. "He decided to come and persuade me to go back to him. After the way I treated him that one time we met on the set, I was surprised to see him."

"You want me to believe you offered him no encouragement, I suppose." The comment died on David's lips as he sank to the leather couch to bury his head in his cupped hands.

Observing him closely, Shelley became aware of his weariness, the sag of his broad shoulders. Lamplight spilled over his open-throated shirt and cast shadows onto his defeated features. The sight stabbed at Shelley's defensive reserve, and for the first time she doubted that she was solely responsible for his weariness and dejection. No, she concluded, for he appeared to be oblivious to her presence, lost in his own deep thoughts and troubles. As if unaware of her scrutiny, he drew his feet up onto the sofa and, uttering a sigh, fell backward against the colorful cushions. Stretching out full length, he closed his eyes. Shelley sensed that he had effectively shut out all outside influences, including her.

She continued to eye him curiously, wondering if he might be deliberately ignoring her, but when several minutes had ticked by, she realized that his seemingly rude silence simply meant he had succumbed to exhausted slumber. Rising from the chair, she approached the sofa. For long, breathless seconds she gazed at his relaxed form and found herself pondering his resemblance to Chris. Odd, she mused; with his features softened by sleep, the similarity seemed less prominent, more of an illusion created by light and shadow. Had it been a figment of her imagination from the very beginning, an image conjured from the depths of her bruised heart that had dwelt too long on the hurts inflicted by Chris? Could she have wanted to meet Chris again, dazzle him with her success and notoriety, her wealth, in order to humble him and bring him to his knees? Had she flaunted her wounded pride like a banner before this man who only slightly resembled Chris? Used him to ease her heartache?

Bending for a closer look, she studied the cleanly defined brow, the bridge of his shapely nose, the firmness of his lips, the smoothness of his jaw. Inspecting his features, she longed to discover traces of dissolution, treachery, reflections of Chris, but there were none. This, she told herself wonderingly, was not the face of a selfish man, a heartless user who preyed upon the tender emotions of lonely women. No, this was the face of a tender man, a man who knew compassion, gentleness and understanding. David's face, not Chris's sardonic visage.

The last remnants of her rage and hatred fled in the instant that Shelley recognized the peaceful countenance as the beloved face of the man she had come to love in a way she had never loved anyone, certainly not Chris Devon. Overcome by a cleansing flood of tenderness, Shelley drew back. What had she said to him in her hurt and anger? Had she blown her last chance to win his respect, if not his love?

Her eyes locked onto David's sleeping face while vivid recollections of their brief time together assaulted her. She relived their stilted meeting on the warm sand of Rehoboth Beach, remembered the moonlit evening that had begun with a verbal sparring match over his knowledge of her identity and ended in a satisfying discussion of her best seller, the discovery of a common understanding and an intellectual bond. As one caught in a time warp, her memories raced forward to the relaxed days and warm friendly nights they had enjoyed at the beach property, skipped happily to his sumptuous New York apartment, to the gala party with its sensually memorable aftermath. Pausing there, she grew warm remembering the degree of passion they had so joyfully shared. She recalled their early days together in Hollywood, his boyish eagerness in guiding her through the maze of studio politics, his almost shy pride in offering this beautiful house to her as a place where she could not only be near him but have time and the uninterrupted solitude so necessary for beginning her new novel.

Theirs had been a good relationship, she concluded, far different from the turbulence she had known with Chris. The lovemaking had been wonderful, at least for her, and David had certainly seemed content. They were relaxed with each other, there was trust, friendship, a meeting of minds . . .

"So you're leaving me, Shelley."

The words sliced through her reflections and jolted her back to the present. Her glance cut to the man who had been sleeping peacefully but who now was awake and observing her through eyes that were bright jewels of accusation.

"Did you mean to go without a word? Were you planning to slip away tonight?" he asked, his beautiful voice devoid of its customary richness. "I suppose you'd arranged to join Devon later? I hope I haven't interrupted some carefully thought-out plan to unite two star-crossed lovers."

"No, no," Shelley argued in a breathless whisper. "I have no plans to meet Chris! Not tonight or ever!" Could she convince him? Make him understand that she loved him and only him?

"I expected you'd say that," he muttered, his voice harsh, his words bitter. "You're forgetting I saw the two of you out there in the garden! A very touching scene, worthy of being a part of *Paradise Unending*. But then, you and Devon have had years of rehearsals to draw upon." His eyes darkened before his lids dropped over them. "I guess I should have known what would hap-

pen when you met him again. It was inevitable."
Dejectedly, he drew himself to a sitting position,
his glittering eyes lifting to impale Shelley's
trembling frame. "Fool that I was, I arranged for
him to play Joshua. It seemed a good choice.
You'd convinced me that we resemble each
other. I didn't see the likeness myself, but I took
your word for it, and once we started working
together, I befriended him, used him for a model
so that I'd give the performance of my life!
That's always been my method of perfecting a
role, you see—I study the character from the
inside out, and I sure studied Devon! My only
mistake, apparently, was letting him know you
were here, alone and anxious to see him again.
When I talked to him earlier tonight, he lit up
like a neon sign."

"You what?" Shelley croaked.

"Aren't you going to thank me, sweet Shelley?" he asked with a rakish grin.

"For what? For getting Chris a part in the
film? He's an actor; it was only a matter of time
before someone in casting considered him," she
stated flatly. "I hope *he* thanked you, but I
imagine he's still the smug bastard he always
was and assumed it was his incredible talent
that got him the part."

David laughed. "He is a bit egotistical, isn't
he? You're right, he never thanked me for any
favors I did him, but I would expect you to be
more appreciative. Devon is a rather pitiful crea-
ture, while you—well, let's say I held you in
higher esteem. I was certain you would be grateful for being reunited with your old love, but—"
He paused, then glanced away as he said in his

normal lilting voice, "I'm willing to express my gratitude to you for writing such a terrific story. To say nothing of the script you managed to convince the studio to use. I've waited all my life for a part like D'Arcy. I'll probably get an Academy Award for playing your degenerate lover in costume." His eyes swung back to her face. Regarding her intently, he mused aloud, "I must admit that I found your lover about as subtle as a rattlesnake. He was an easy study for me, but not the sort of man I expected a woman like you to lose her head over."

His narrowed eyes raked her flimsily clad body, paused appreciatively on her upthrust breasts before moving on to her rounded hips and long legs silhouetted by the lamplight gleaming through the gossamer fabric of her simple robe. "I gave you credit, Shelley, for being a modern woman, intelligent and savvy, but I was wrong, wasn't I? I took one look at you and I was hooked. I've known lots of beautiful women, even thought I was in love with a few, but I'd never seen anybody like you, with your face of an angel, body of a goddess and that quicksilver temper. That was before I realized you were *the* Shelley Tremayne, not her daughter or her sister or whatever. You'll probably never believe me, but from the first reading of that book, I figured the author was some middle-aged frustrated frump pouring out her erotic longings to earn a fast buck. When I discovered the truth, I was impressed. I figured you had it all together. After years of looking for just the right woman, I thought I'd found the perfect combination of beauty, intelligence and total

femininity. How could I know you were a push-
over for the wrong men?"

"You arranged for Chris to be hired?" Shelley
asked, ignoring his insolent glance, his sneering
remarks.

"I said I did, didn't I?" he replied. "I asked the
casting office to offer him the part for more than
one reason, I have to admit. I wanted to meet the
great Chris Devon, see him up close, observe
him, learn from him, find out what kind of man
you wanted."

He was going too fast for her. She was still
considering his earlier remarks. "You told him I
was anxious to see him again? What made you
think that?"

"Oh, come on! I'd read your book, listened to
you when you told me all about the two of you,
saw the haunted look in your eyes." He paused to
regard her through narrowed eyes. "I still can't
figure it out. As soon as he showed up on the set,
I saw him for what he was. I couldn't . . . can't,"
he amended quickly, "believe you can't see that
he's a hard-core phony and not the romantic
dream lover you've created in your own mind.
The woman I thought you were would have
relegated him to the trash pile of has-beens
where he belongs, but it didn't work out that
way."

"David, what are you implying?"

"Implying?" he snorted. "I'm not implying
anything! I'm calling it the way I see it, love."
His dark glance impaled her as he explained
caustically, "I played the Peeping Tom and
watched that tender little scene between you
and Devon. It seems I've done you one hell of a

favor." He rose to his feet and commenced to pace restlessly.

Terrified and confused, Shelley observed him in silence, waited for an opportunity to speak in her own defense.

Suddenly he halted and swung toward her. "You've been reunited with your heart's desire and now you're ready to dump me, isn't that the way it is? What we had means nothing to you, does it? I'm just another actor climbing to the top of the heap, but not *the* actor who holds the key to your heart," he said angrily. "Why didn't I foresee this development? Why did I delude myself into thinking I'd come out ahead? God, it's just like it used to be! I've come so far only to take ten steps back."

"What are you talking about?" Shelley, at a loss to comprehend his meaning, found her voice.

"I've just realized that you don't know much about me," he said quietly. "Got a minute before you rush off into the night?"

Thoroughly baffled, Shelley nodded her head and waited to hear whatever he might be about to say.

"Once you asked me a question I didn't answer because I didn't think it was important. I'm going to answer you now."

"David, you're talking in riddles," she said.

"Maybe, but I'll try to make it short," he assured her. Hands thrust deep into the pockets of his trousers, he kept his back to her while he talked of things that were clearly painful to him. "As I recall, we were talking about Hollywood and my career. I told you I'd done some awful movies that paid good money, but that once I'd proven myself, I decided to be more careful in accepting roles. You asked me who I was trying to prove myself to." Glancing over his shoulder, he caught her puzzled glance and said, "Remember?"

"Yes," she said, remembering clearly the night they had sat in her beach cottage conversing with the companionable ease of good friends.

"All my life, I've had to win approval from somebody. First, it was my family. Ambitious achievers, all of them. My mother was the driving force. She wasn't satisfied that I was happy as an actor—she wanted me to be *the* actor at the top of the heap. She didn't live long enough to see me fulfill her expectations." He sighed before going on. "Then there was the studio, who picked my roles, my dates and even where I lived. When I wanted out of my contract, they put me in those monster movies for punishment. That backfired and I was able to make a name for myself, and now nobody puts me down." He sucked in a deep breath and swung around to face her. "Nobody has dared to until now."

"Now?"

"In choosing Devon over me, you're putting me down," he said with grim quietness.

"What on earth are you talking about? What makes you think I've chosen Chris?"

Ignoring her tortured question, he grinned broadly and said, "So it's off with the new and on with the old—lover, that is. Where will you go with your Romeo? Somewhere bright and expensive, I'll bet. Your paramour is the sort who aims high, even when he lands in the gutter—as he always does, doesn't he? You do understand, don't you, that it's your money he's interested in? Are you prepared to support him in the grand manner he prefers?"

"Oh, David, you don't actually believe I'd go back with Chris, do you?" she asked incredulously.

"Why not? Isn't he everything you've always wanted? The only man you've ever wanted? The inspiration for your first book?" His voice, low and insinuating, whined in her ears as he continued to talk in that derogatory tone that was a carefully studied imitation of Chris's voice.

Unable to bear his hurtful accusations, his snide stabs, Shelley clamped her hands over her ears and cried hysterically, "Stop! Stop it! Stop talking like him, using his voice, his mannerisms! Don't you know what you're doing? You've become so like him, you're driving me insane!"

His head reared back, his bright eyes swept ruthlessly over her, but he said no more. As if recognizing that his sharp thrusts had struck with unfailing accuracy, he grew quiet. Running his fingers restlessly through his thick thatch of hair, he seemed contrite and uncharacteristically awkward.

Shelley regarded him warily as she fought to subdue her pain, the agony of her spirit, and wondered if he knew he had inflicted fresh and exceedingly deep wounds to her heart. Maybe it was deserved, she reflected, remembering her own past attempts at deflating his ego, the wrongs she had attributed to him.

"Oh, God!" he groaned, his long strides bringing him to her side. His arms reached for her, gathered her close. Folding her in a tender embrace, he rocked her gently. "Forgive me, Shelley, forgive me, my love," he crooned quietly. "I didn't know, I truly didn't know. I felt terrible when I heard you say you were leaving! I think I went a little crazy myself. All I wanted to do was hurt you as you'd hurt me! It was bad enough when I saw you with him and I thought—"

"You thought wrong!" Shelley argued between heart-wrenching sobs. "You saw something that wasn't there. I despise him, can't stand the sight of him, the sound of his voice. And you . . . you've become so like him . . . his voice comes from your throat, you've adopted his mannerisms . . . you've changed into him! What you said about him, it's all true, every word of it! I found that out years ago, and my memory hasn't failed me no matter what you think! He's weak and vain and vile and he said things about you, hinted that you plan to dump me," she choked, "so I figured it was best to leave before you got the chance to . . ."

Cupping her head with one hand, he stroked the rumpled silkiness of her hair and said, "When I saw you in the garden, I assumed you had reconciled with him. What was I to think?"

"What he wanted you to think," she replied curtly, swallowing back her salty tears. "He's not the great actor he thinks he is, but he is an actor and he staged that whole scene. He even had me feeling sorry for him for a while. When he got here, he told me you were still on the set. But I'll bet he knew you were here. It wouldn't surprise me if he had followed you home!" It was all terrifyingly clear in her mind's eye; Chris had probably followed at a safe distance, waited for the gates to open so that he could slip inside behind David's car. David, weary and anxious to be free of the studio, would not have noticed a second car, especially if the lights were doused and the driver cruising in the glow of the lead car. "He came here to create a scene," she mused aloud, "to cause more trouble for me . . . for us."

"Hush, Shelley, hush!" David whispered. His thumb teased the tense muscles of her set jaw; his forefinger traced the trembling softness of her lips. "Whatever he said about me doesn't matter. He knows nothing about me except what I allowed him to know, and I'm guilty of fabricating now and then for press releases and to bewilder people I don't like."

Tilting her head backward, Shelley gazed up into his face. "You said you befriended Chris, and yet you don't know how sly and devious he can be! Don't you know how he can twist things to his own design?"

"Yes, Shelley, I know. I just didn't realize you knew it," he said with a fond smile. "He's already spreading rather sordid rumors about sweet little Jenny Sinclair. The girl is too young and trusting to realize what's happening, but she's learning, toughening, rolling with the punches."

"Stories about Jenny? And you?"

"Some of the stories are about the two of us. I've denied everything, of course. I've also put out some tales of my own, hinted that I'm about to settle down with someone outside the business, omitted names but given the press something to print besides Devon's lies."

Shelley's heart seemed to stop as she listened to his remarks. She had to know, had to ask, "Is it true? I mean, are you thinking of settling down? Is there somebody . . . ?" She couldn't finish, was unable to form the word "else" for fear he would affirm her worst fears.

He smiled enigmatically. "Maybe there is and maybe there isn't. What difference does it make so long as the press has something to speculate about?"

It wasn't exactly the reply she had expected, but she sensed that pressing him would only lead to embarrassment. "And Jenny? Are you going to allow Chris to ruin her life? Her career, maybe?"

"I've given her a few pointers on fielding bad press, but I'm not going to put myself in the middle. Jenny has a bright future and she's learning to defend herself. Now, enough shop talk."

Emphasizing his determination, he placed his mouth to hers in a kiss of such devastating sweetness that it erased all thoughts of the studio and Jenny Sinclair's precarious predicament. As the caress deepened to heated passion, the lingering memories of Chris were swept away on a wave of longing for the man holding her in familiar arms. Deep within her, hot desire uncoiled, rose and spread upward from her aching loins until all her senses were afire. Wrapping her arms around David, she molded her curves to his hard body. Clinging to him, Shelley returned his agonizingly tender caresses with a wildness born of need and remembered desire. Her eager tongue met his invading roughness, entwined with it, while her hands explored, remembered, aroused, rekindled. Her writhing hips teased, invited, encouraged, beckoned and were matched by flanks that frankly welcomed the advances.

Neither could have said who made the first move, whose desire was greater, whose moans more desperate. It didn't seem to matter as Shelley found herself bending effortlessly backward beneath the weightlessness of David's body. Hands moved with agile quickness and clothes slipped willingly from heated flesh. Hungry mouths clung; tongues met with avid abandon. As their feverishly entwined bodies sank to the thickly carpeted floor, Shelley realized her lower half was completely enveloped by David, her long legs trapped between his so that she was achingly aware of his need.

With bare flesh pressed eagerly to bare flesh, his lips trailed fire, worshiped nipples that became raw pinpoints of sensitivity. His fingers feathered, roamed, roused, ignited until passion radiated outward from their burning core. Shelley's breasts tingled from the touch of David's hair-roughened chest. Arching against him, she exulted in the tremor that assaulted her thighs. When his body shifted so that he was astride her, she gazed dreamily into his passion-glazed eyes and saw her own reflection there, the image of a woman ready to receive the love of her man.

Unhurriedly, he began an arousing exploration of her naked flesh with his hands. His eyes held hers as his fingertips moved with worshipful lightness over her swollen breasts, down along the gentle slope of her belly to the secret regions of her desire. He smiled as she gasped in erotic torment. Her nerves vibrated and screamed. When she would have cried out in sensual anguish, he bent to brush his lips lightly against hers.

With her patience growing short, she commenced her own exploration of his firm muscularity. Her fingers trailed lightly over his shoulders, across his smooth chest, toyed with the vee of hair, following its dwindling path to the source of his virility. His rasping gasp was her reward as she offered her shameless invitation, one he did not reject as he moved until his hard body was atop hers. For only a moment, he paused. Then he was inside her, filling her, plunging deeper and deeper into the receptive recesses of her sweetness.

Legs wrapped around his, Shelley rode the waves of ecstasy. Passion pounded in her blood, through her heart, her brain. Sensation followed sensation, cresting on higher and higher peaks of rapture, and she knew she was not alone in her erotic realm of pleasure. David's body rose and fell in rhythm with hers until their bodies achieved an exquisite harmony.

When they at last lay quiet, exhaustedly content, Shelley turned her eyes to his and was startled to find their aquamarine brilliance unblinkingly fixed on her flushed face. Snaking her hand upward, she cupped his smooth-shaven jaw and said, "I love you, David Warren. I fought it, but it wouldn't go away. I love you."

There, she had actually said it. She avoided his eyes for fear of seeing rejection reflected there.

David smiled tenderly. "And I love you, Shelley Tremayne. I think I've loved you since I first saw you on the beach trembling with fear of Fritz and Karl. Once I found out that we were two of a kind, I was sure you were the only woman for me."

"You love me? I'm the only woman for you?" It was too good to be true, she exulted, as her heart thundered against her rib cage. She must have misunderstood him. Oh! If only he would say it again! Then she would know she was not dreaming.

Clasping the hand cupping his chin, he raised it to his lips. "Yes, I love you. I love everything about you. I'd be a fool not to love your beauty, your incredible body and the way it responds to mine. I adore the way we think alike and enjoy the quiet things of life. Would you believe, I even love your stubbornness, your quicksilver temper, and I worship your exceptional talent."

"My talent?" she echoed, flustered by the intensity of his eyes, the husky sincerity of his declaration.

"Your writing. You wrote one terrific novel and screenplay, in case it's slipped your mind."

"I might have known," Shelley said playfully. "You're an actor first, last and always. You just want me to write you more award-winning roles!"

"No, not really. I want you, not your work. I don't care if I never star in another Shelley Tremayne story again. We shot my death scene this afternoon, in fact. Rather apropos, don't you think?"

"How so?"

"The death of Lord D'Arcy, the symbolic burial of Chris Devon," he said with teasing lightness. "The rebirth of David Warren, the man who loves Shelley Tremayne. The man, Shelley, not the actor. My love for you isn't an act."

Smiling, David leaned over her and whispered, "We're two of a kind, Shelley, did you know that? We've both been used by the worst sort of people. Do you think we can overcome that sort of thing and trust each other?"

"We can try, David," she replied, as he rained soft kisses against her forehead. "How can I prove that I do love you, that I'll never stop loving you? Do you want me to live with you, give up my writing except for screenplays that will suit you, devote myself only to you?"

Lowering himself until he lay atop her soft curves, he chuckled, "I'd never ask you to give up your writing. You're too good to become my personal playright. As for living together, what would that prove? I thought we've been living together." He kissed her again, his tongue tracing the moist outline of her lips, his fingertips teasing the soft swell of her breast, but when she eagerly responded, he drew back. "No doubt about it, we do have a marvelous body chemistry, but I don't think living together's the best answer, Shelley. Any other ideas?"

Shelley pretended to be considering as she savored the warmth of his mouth, tasted the tangy saltiness of him with the tip of her tongue and let her hands roam curiously over the smoothness of his skin. "I don't have too many ideas left, David," she said slowly, her tongue teasing his male nipples between the halting words.

"And you a writer? What good is a writer who's run out of ideas?" he countered, his hands moving magically, lightly over her nakedness.

"I'm just an old-fashioned girl raised on a farm in Michigan. Back there, the way people prove their love is by marrying and putting up with each other year in and year out. Does that work in California and Rehoboth Beach?" she asked innocently.

David's head lifted; his eyes captured her gaze and held it. "Are you asking me to marry you, Shelley?"

"It's only a suggestion," she said, raising one shapely shoulder negligently. "I read somewhere that marriage is coming back into fashion. We could try it, I suppose, if you're agreeable."

"Well . . ." he said, playing at shrewdness, "that sounds pretty good, but what more can you offer?"

"A lifetime of love," she said quietly, sincerely. "If you're looking for fringe benefits, I promise to share your life." Still David played the skeptic. Taking a deep breath, she said with exaggerated resignation, "Okay, I'll let all our children attend acting academies so they can follow in your footsteps. We'll establish a dynasty like the Barrymores. It's my last offer. What do you think?"

He gathered her into his arms and whispered, "A dynasty of my own? That's an offer I can't refuse. But I'm warning you, I'll give you only fifty or sixty years to fulfill all those promises." A whimsical smile curved his lips.

"Then you will marry me? For better or for worse?"

"I will," he said solemnly. "To prove I'm sincere, I'll even set a date for the wedding. Can you wait until the movie has been wrapped up and we go back to Rehoboth? Fritz and Karl can be our witnesses, okay? Honeymoon at the beach?" At her enthusiastic nod, he sighed and said, "In the meantime, I've got some heavy work to do."

"Oh?"

"I have to prove to the world's number one best-selling author that I'm a worthwhile catch. How do you see my chances of convincing her?"

"I'd say they're very good if you don't waste a lot of time talking. After all, you've got to get started on that dynasty if it's ever going to be a reality," she whispered, molding her body to his and covering his mouth with lips that were determined to aid him in the persuasion.

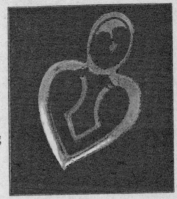

Silhouette Special Edition. Romances
for the woman who expects a little
more out of love.

If you enjoyed this book, and you're ready for more great romance

...get 4 romance novels FREE when you become a Silhouette Special Edition home subscriber.

Act now and we'll send you four exciting Silhouette Special
Edition romance novels. They're our gift to introduce you to our
convenient home subscription service. Every month, we'll send
you six new passion-filled Special Edition books. Look them
over for 15 days. If you keep them, pay just $11.70 for all six. Or
return them at no charge.

We'll mail your books to you two full months *before they are
available anywhere else.* Plus, with every shipment, you'll receive
the Silhouette Books Newsletter absolutely free. *And with
Silhouette Special Edition there are never any shipping or handling charges.*

Mail the coupon today to get your four free books—and more
romance than you ever bargained for.

Silhouette Special Edition is a service mark and a registered trademark.

Enjoy romance and passion, larger-than-life...

Now, thrill to 4 Silhouette Intimate Moments novels (a $9.00 value) — ABSOLUTELY FREE!

If you want more passionate sensual romance, then Silhouette Intimate Moments novels are for you!

In every 256-page book, you'll find romance that's electrifying...involving... and intense. And now, these larger-than-life romances can come into your home every month!

4 FREE books as your introduction.

Act now and we'll send you four thrilling Silhouette Intimate Moments novels. They're our gift to introduce you to our convenient home subscription service. Every month, we'll send you four new Silhouette Intimate Moments books. Look them over for 15 days. If you keep them, pay just $9.00 for all four. Or return them at no charge.

We'll mail your books to you *as soon as they are published.* Plus, with every shipment, you'll receive the Silhouette Books Newsletter absolutely free. *And Silhouette Intimate Moments is delivered free.*

Mail the coupon today and start receiving Silhouette Intimate Moments. Romance novels for women...not girls.

Silhouette Intimate Moments

Silhouette Intimate Moments™
120 Brighton Road, P.O. Box 5084, Clifton, N.J. 07015-5084

☐ **YES!** Please send me FREE and without obligation, 4 exciting Silhouette Intimate Moments romance novels. Unless you hear from me after I receive my 4 FREE books, please send 4 new Silhouette Intimate Moments novels to preview each month. I understand that you will bill me $2.25 each for a total of $9.00—with no additional shipping, handling or other charges. **There is no minimum number of books to buy and I may cancel anytime I wish.** The first 4 books are mine to keep, even if I never take a single additional book.

☐ Mrs. ☐ Miss ☐ Ms. ☐ Mr.   BMS225

Name	(please print)
Address	Apt. #
City	State	Zip
( )	
Area Code	Telephone Number

Signature (if under 18, parent or guardian must sign)

This offer, limited to one per customer. Terms and prices subject
to change. Your enrollment is subject to acceptance by Silhouette Books.

SILHOUETTE INSPIRATIONS is a trademark and service mark.

IM-OP-A

READERS' COMMENTS ON SILHOUETTE SPECIAL EDITIONS:

"I just finished reading the first six Silhouette Special Edition Books and I had to take the opportunity to write you and tell you how much I enjoyed them. I enjoyed all the authors in this series. Best wishes on your Silhouette Special Editions line and many thanks."

—B.H.*, Jackson, OH

"The Special Editions are really special and I enjoyed them very much! I am looking forward to next month's books."

—R.M.W.*, Melbourne, FL

"I've just finished reading four of your first six Special Editions and I enjoyed them very much. I like the more sensual detail and longer stories. I will look forward each month to your new Special Editions."

—L.S.*, Visalia, CA

"Silhouette Special Editions are — 1.) Superb! 2.) Great! 3.) Delicious! 4.) Fantastic! . . . Did I leave anything out? These are books that an adult woman can read . . . I love them!"

—H.C.*, Monterey Park, CA

*names available on request